A Different Kind of Hero

D0062482

A Different Kind of Hero

by Ann R. Blakeslee

Marshall Cavendish

New York

Text copyright © 1997 by Ann R. Blakeslee
Marshall Cavendish, 99 White Plains Road, Tarrytown, New York 10591
The text of this book is set in 12 point Bembo
Book design by Constance Ftera
First Marshall Cavendish Paperbacks edition 2003
Printed in the United States of America

Library of Congress Cataloging-in-Publication Data
Blakeslee, Ann R.
A different kind of hero / by Ann R. Blakeslee.
p.   cm.
Summary: In 1881 twelve-year-old Renny, who resists his father's efforts
to turn him into a rough, tough, brawling boy, earns the disapproval of the
entire mining camp when he befriends a newly arrived Chinese boy.
ISBN 0-7614-5147-1
[1. Frontier and pioneer life—West (U.S.)—Fiction. 2. West (U.S.)—Fiction.
3. Chinese Americans—Fiction. 4. Fathers and sons—Fiction.] I. Title.
PZ7.B577Di   1977   [Fic]—dc20   96-32786   CIP   AC

1   3   5   7   8   6   4   2

This book is dedicated to
Merritt, Christopher, Joel, Edith and Quentin
who make mothering my favorite career.

Contents

1

Trouble!

Night. Cold. I buttoned my coat and took the sack Mr. McMinn held out. "Run with it and they'll likely smother," he said, his lips curled in a teasing smile around his cigar. "Then you won't mind dropping them in the creek." When I didn't answer, he shook his head. "You're the strangest lad ever worked here. Most wouldn't give drowning three worthless pups a second thought."

I held one hand under the sack to stop it swinging. "Doesn't seem fair, them so young."

"What's not fair is what it'll cost to feed 'em, are they not done away with. Go along now." Trailing cigar smoke, he stalked back into the office of the livery stable and slammed the door.

Main Street traffic hummed past me. The boardwalks on either side, lit with lanterns, rang hollow under tramping boots. Miners poured toward saloons and boardinghouses, the day shift at the camp's two gold mines having ended. I saw my da just ahead. Deep in talk, not watching where he trod, he rammed into a man striding toward him. The man bellowed, "Why don't you dirty miners keep to the street?"

"And let you swells hog the boardwalks?" Da bellowed back.

Somebody laid a hand on the man's shoulder, maybe warning him to go careful with Da. He pushed the hand off. "Next time one of you swipes against me," he roared, "I'll knock him winding."

"Why not now?" Da roared in reply. Seeing a crowd gather, the man turned to go but Da caught his arm and whirled him back.

A chant started and rose louder, "Go, Lon, go," the insult to one Irish miner being taken as a insult to them all.

The crowd poured into the street, pulling Da and the other man with them. Drivers, unable to pass, tied their reins and stood in their drays and wagons to watch. I could see naught of Da but his black cap as he put up his hands to settle it in place. His opponent was easier to follow, him being taller. He was dark-haired under a silk hat, shaved close except for the drooping mustache he gnawed as he slid off his coat.

Mr. McMinn's sack twisted in my hand, the pups kicking and whining. I made sure its string was knotted and set it under the boardwalk so it wouldn't get trampled. Then, because Da'd want me there cheering him on, I butted through the ring of watching men. Oh Da, I was thinking, couldn't you have talked out your difference? Why settle everything with a fight?

The miners made way when they saw who was pushing in. They all knew me, Lon Sholto's boy, Renny. Were always making a compliment of saying I looked just like him, green-eyed, freckled-faced, black-haired as we both were. Kept asking me was I a scrapper like him? Likely knew I wasn't.

The man Da fought wore shiny shoes and a striped waistcoat. Usually that kind folded when a fist was raised but this one knew how to fight. He struck his blows solid, didn't panic like some. Already Da bled from a cut along his jaw. "Who is it Da fights?" I asked the man beside me.

"Came in on the afternoon coach from Denver. Met with the owner of the Kitkat mine. Now he's meeting the Kitkat miners." He laughed.

Da struck with his left, hitting the other in the face. The man shook his head and blinked but one eyelid hung shut. Da crashed his right to the man's stomach. His opponent thrust back. Da whipped his face away, catching the blow above his ear. Their punches kept landing so hard I ached like 'twas my body they pummeled.

Then the stranger seemed to tire, moved slower, puffing. Da danced in jabbing left and right but not striking, watching to see if the other was about to call it quits. But quick as a trap snaps, Da's foe pulled a narrow knife from his sleeve and held it at arm's length, the point to Da's throat. "Don't," I yelled. A miner jerked me back lest I interfere. But he feared for Da, too, I could tell. His breath hissed in dread.

"Stay away from me, you mine rat," snarled the stranger through set teeth. The crowd fell so silent I heard the piano playing up at the dance hall.

Da dropped his hands and did as he was bade, taking a step back. I thought to turn my eyes away lest I shame him, watching him lose. But I had to see.

Then, quicker than the man pulled the knife, Da's foot came up kicking it from his grasp. The man paled. Da shot his hard hands round his foe's throat and shook him till he sagged. "Now then," Da asked, "who are you, thinking to shout Lon Sholto off the boardwalk?"

The man rolled his eyes, looking for help, but who'd speak for one that pulled a knife in a fistfight? At last the answer strangled out, "The owner at the Kitkat Mine sought advice about cheap labor. Cheap labor is my business."

"Well, listen careful, Mr. Cheap Labor," Da said. "I'll carve you with your own knife 'less you climb on that stagecoach and stay put till it pulls out tomorrow. Don't go signaling for help. You'll be watched."

The man rubbed his throat, picked up his hat and coat and brushed through the crowd, head bowed as though he studied his shiny shoes. Da jerked a thumb at two of the miners and they trailed after.

The others slapped Da's back, laughing over how easy he'd won. Easy! Hadn't death reached out for Da and barely missed? The miners hoisted him on their shoulders and carried him off toward Irish Gulch. Little Lon

Sholto, their hero, who'd fight anybody came down the pike.

I got Mr. McMinn's sack and walked to the creek holding it close. The pups cried and struggled inside. I started to untie it but didn't. Why kill them? Maybe somebody'd take them tomorrow. Tonight, once everybody got to sleep, I'd put them behind the stove so the night cold wouldn't freeze the life out of them.

When I got home Da was telling Mam about his win as she dabbed arnica on his cuts. My sisters stood watching. "You tell them, boyo," said he, "how your old da bested the city swell."

I told it all, each blow, knowing from times past that he'd set me straight if I forgot a single thrust or sidestep. "Then they raised Da to their shoulders like a king and all cheered as they carried him past."

"And where were you?" he asked. "Another boy'd have been capering alongside bragging that was his da."

"Doing a chore for Mr. McMinn." That satisfied him. Almost.

"Don't you ever again cry out when I'm fighting. You hear me?"

"Yes, Da."

"Why not?" six-year-old Nora asked.

"It jars my mind off what I'm doing. And it sounds like he doubts I'll win." That struck so close to the truth I held my breath. But Mam set the stewpot on the table and the fight was forgot.

Hours later I woke sitting upright. Da's oaths shook

our night-black cabin like thunder. "Nora," he shouted up the ladder, "are these your blasted pups piddling on the floor for me to step in?"

"No, Da." She went to wailing.

"Bridget?" he asked my big sister.

"Of course not."

"Renny, get down here." I started struggling into my trousers but he said, "Now!" Down the loft ladder I climbed in my nightshirt, shivering from cold and fear of what he'd do. I'd meant to get those pups outside before anyone woke up.

Da held the lantern high. The pups had hid but a whimper came from behind the woodbox. "I hoped it wasn't you brought these pesky pups in, but should have known 'twas. Haven't you come dragging broken-winged birds, stray cats, kids, and beggars home since you could toddle, thinking I'd be glad to feed them?"

Being yelled at by him in his nightclothes, his curls and beard awry from sleep, hairy feet bare, made what I'd done seem extra sinful. "Yes, Da. I'm sorry. I was meaning to find somebody to take them in."

"Hoping you'd persuade me to, more like. Round them up and toss them outside. If they live till daybreak, get them back where they came from."

"I can't. Mr. McMinn doesn't want them. He said to drop them in the creek."

"Why didn't you, then?"

"I couldn't send them under the ice yowling and choking and scrabbling for a place to cling to."

"You'll see worse than that. Bridget, throw your brother's boots down." I looked up and saw my sisters' pale faces afloat in the dark at the edge of the loft. Then the boots landed so close to Da's feet he had to jump back. "Bridget Mary Sholto!" he bellowed, but he never could cow her. She stared back at him as calm as though he hadn't spoke.

When I'd got the boots on he said, "Lay the ax on the chopping block and come get these varmints." Vomit rose in my throat. Would he chop off their heads or make me?

"Not the ax, Lon." Mam spoke at last from the bed.

"Why not?" asked Da. "Should a man be waylaid in the dark of his own cabin by messing pups? What if he takes pity on rattlesnakes next?"

"I'll see he doesn't," Mam said. "Gather up those pups, Renny. Get rid of them however you want. Now!"

"Like this?" I asked, having on so few clothes.

"Like that, to remind you to think before you act."

It wasn't easy catching the pups, small though they were. I pulled one from behind the water bucket, the others from under the stove, and let them down into the sack I'd brought them in. "Can't we keep one?" Nora asked.

"No!"

"Just one. The littlest . . ."

While she tangled Da in questions I lifted the latch, thinking to slip away unnoticed. But he shouted after me, "Twelve years old and too softhearted to drown

15

pups! Bridget would have thought nothing of doing it. You'd best toughen up, boyo. It's not long until you'll be at work underground. The mines grind weaklings to dust."

A wind howled outside, so cold my throat ached and my body longed for cover. I didn't loose the pups near the cabin lest Da decide to prove how tough he was by crushing them underfoot. They cried and complained, the sack heavier with every step as I made my way to Main Street.

When I got there I surveyed the boardwalks. Any man still around would likely feel as Da did about the pups. Anyway, in my nightshirt, how could I go asking? I stood undecided until the cold drove me to action. I ran behind the stores to the house the dance hall girls lived in. They were said to have soft hearts.

Their place had real glass windows like the mine owners' and storekeepers' homes down on Main Street. Lamps shone out a welcome. I tried the door and it opened. I set the sack inside. Somebody called but I didn't wait to see what 'twas they wanted.

When I reached home 'twas hard lifting the latch, so stiff were my hands. I fell asleep wondering about Da and me. Different as I was from the roughneck he thought I ought to be, could I ever make him proud?

We slept late next morning. Da rushed off to the Kitkat without breakfast, lunch bucket in one hand, a half loaf in the other. I lingered in the loft till he'd gone, not wanting to set him off again.

We gulped our porridge, except Nora, who could

make one meal last until the next one. Mam, plaiting up her long, gold hair, lectured as I ate. "Don't be so head-long today. Think through to the outcome before you plunge into something. And don't judge your da. He's harsh because he wants the best for you." I wasn't sure she had that last part right.

Bridgey hurried off to school when her friend Doreen came knocking. I filled the water pails at the creek and carried in stove wood. Then Nora and I left, Mam calling after us to run.

"We'd best take the shortcut," I said. "Teacher's been at me all week. She'd love me coming tardy so she could send me to the punishment stool."

"But Mam says never to take the shortcut in April."

"We'd have heard if bears were out," I said. "Anyway, I'd rather face a bear than Teacher riled up."

We cut up behind the houses, following the icy mountain path that led past the gold camp's rubbish heap to the school. Mist hung like ghosts between the trees. "Are there any bear tracks?" Nora asked, peering around. I took her hand.

A bluejay gave its sandpaper call from a branch above us, then shot past, startling Nora so she skidded and fell, pulling me after. I scrambled up and set her on her feet, wiping her tears on my sleeve, then went more careful, watching not to trip over roots. When I looked up I flung my arms out.

Right ahead lay the little meadow the camp dumped rubbish in. Ravens pecked around it muttering and squawking. Among them shouldered a black bear, a female with two cubs. I was too scared to think. All I knew was, Nora had to be got away safe. I clamped my hand across her mouth and held her tight, her whole body athrob with fear like a deer mouse you drop in your pocket.

Her red shawl burned bright as fire in that dark forest. I whispered, "Let loose your shawl. I'll shove it under my coat lest it catch the eye of the bear." She did as I bade.

I thought first to send her back toward Main Street but moving back was as chancy as moving ahead. I waited to be certain the bear hadn't seen us before letting her loose. With my lips at her ear I warned, "Should you screech, the bear'll be on us, to protect her cubs." Then, going slow, I pushed her farther into the trees that bounded the meadow. There was no underbrush to hide us, just skinny trunks of tall pines. A chill wind blew in our faces, carrying our scent away from the bear.

The cubs wrestled together. Their mother grunted and snuffled through the piled trash. I whispered, "You go on. Follow the dip in the snow that shows where the path runs. I'll come when you're far enough away to be safe." She shook her head, biting her lip. Tears coursed down her cheeks. I pushed her and raised my fist like I meant to hit her, though she must have known I wouldn't. At last she set off looking so small it made my heart ache.

She had taken but seven steps when the wind shifted. The bear raised her head, sniffed and let out a roar that bounded from the cliffs, rumbling and growing. The terrible sound froze us where we stood. Ravens flapped into the air, squawking hoarse like their throats were sore. I prayed their noise would claim the bear's attention but it didn't. She reared onto her hind legs and peered toward the trees where we cowered. Her front paw was raised, mouth open, her breath a cloud between her yellow teeth.

Sobs tore Nora's throat. Cold though 'twas, sweat ran down my back. Icicles clinked on the bear's fur like warning bells telling us not to move. Nora's eyes locked with mine, saying the last good-by she daren't speak aloud.

Then the wind veered again. With a lingering look and a last few sniffs toward us, the bear dropped down and began pushing garbage around with her pointed nose. Nora was willing to run ahead, then. She slithered and slid up the slope, gasping and looking behind every few steps. I stood steeling myself to stand forward and be mauled if need be. When Nora was almost out of sight and the bear had shown no sign she knew we were there, I followed after.

We stopped in the schoolyard so Nora could have a good cry. She clung to me. Then, like the sun came out she grinned and said, "Wait till the kids hear what we did. Their eyes'll pop."

"We can't tell, not anybody," I said, wrapping her shawl around her. "Promise."

I don't think she heard me. "They'll pester so I'll have to tell it over and over."

"Word of a bear will fly through the camp like wild-fire. Da will hear of it. He'll strike me dead for putting you in danger. You know he will. And Mam will be as mad because I didn't look ahead to what could happen."

My words were wasted. "I bet Bridgey'd have run crying. We're braver than her. I'll put that in."

I shook her. "Listen! It's got to be kept quiet, though I hate it as much as you. If we could tell, Da'd see I'm not the coward he thinks." She stopped smiling. "Please," I begged her, "keep it a secret to save me getting beat past bearing." She wiped her nose on her mitten and worried the fringe on her shawl, making up her mind. At last she took a deep breadth and crossed her heart.

"You're mean. I hate you," she said and stalked into school stamping her feet.

So late were we that the Bible reading was over and they were already singing the times tables. Miss Steele held up her hand to halt them. "What is the meaning of this late arrival?"

Would Nora tell? I couldn't blame her if the secret spilled out. Instead of answering she burst into tears again though I'd thought she'd already used up all the tears she had. Lifting her skirts, she showed her torn stockings where she'd fallen. Miss Steele tsk-tsked and waved her to her bench and me to the punishment stool.

I knew she'd question me later. I went to work on what I'd say. She'd not hear about those bears from me.

2

The Intruders

Late that morning I was still perched on the punishment stool. Teacher hadn't found time yet to give me my talking-to. When feet stamped on the mat outside the schoolhouse door, I turned to see who was coming.

"Stop gaping, Renny," Miss Steele snapped. Her mind wasn't really on me, though. She was straightening the paper cuffs she wore to keep her sleeves clean. Then she went to pinning her black hair tighter, getting slicked up before whoever was outside came in.

The door squealed open and two people stepped through. When I saw who they were I knew there'd be trouble. Sure enough, the teacher's cheeks turned an angry red and her lips went tight. She jumped to her feet, her long black skirt swishing.

Finn Brodie whispered loud enough for all to hear, "They got their nerve, coming here."

But Nora slid off her bench and went and smiled up at the strangers. "Pretty," she said, touching a dragon embroidered on the man's sleeve. The other five- and six-year-olds copied her, "Pretty, pretty."

Miss Steele slapped her ruler against the big wooden box she used for a desk. "Nora! Return to your seat at once!" Nora did as Teacher said, slowly, walking backward. "What do you want?" Miss Steele asked the intruders though the answer was plain, the boy standing there with a slate under his arm.

The Chinese who'd come in were the first ever seen in our gold camp. The widow lady who was the new owner of the Rejoice Mine brought them with her from California to run her house and cook her meals. They'd been around camp lately, dressed in baggy blue pants and shirts, everybody watching them, pretending not to. That morning, though, the man had on a yellow robe woven over with strange animals. In his good clothes, all gold and colors, he didn't look like somebody's servant.

His kid wore knickers and a shirt, tie and jacket like all us boys except his were newer. His shiny, high-buttoned shoes squeaked when he stepped across the dirt floor to ask Miss Steele, "May I introduce my father, Mr. Wong Gum? I myself am Wong Gum Zi." They bowed. Their long black pigtails slithered across their shoulders and dropped down to swing beside their faces.

"Like snakes," Sis Paunce said out loud. Because her da owned the Kitkat gold mine, making him boss of half the miners in camp, she always felt free to poke fun.

The Chinese boy went on like she hadn't spoke, "For two years I attended school in San Francisco, and last year in the gold camp at Indian Branch. I hope to continue my schooling here in Colorado so

22

that I may become an American boy."

His English was better than most of ours in the log schoolhouse that April day in 1881. Them who talked Welsh or German or Polish at home had accents that made Miss Steele frown with vexation. Some days she wouldn't even call on any of us from Irish Gulch. To rest her ears, she said, from the way we wrung out the language.

The teacher's answer to the Chinese boy burst out, "What you ask is impertinent! Impossible!" She waved him away with her ruler. "We want no Orientals here. Get along now, both of you."

The visitors talked together in their own jangly language. Then the boy said to Miss Steele, "Please await the arrival of my mistress, Mrs. Maynard. My father says she will come to discuss this matter with you." He bowed and his da bowed behind him. Sis gave her scornful giggle as they turned and left.

School hadn't been that exciting since a dynamite blast at Mr. Paunce's Kitkat Mine toppled the stovepipe, choking us with soot. Everybody had to talk about those Chinese. Miss Steele rapped till she got us quiet. She took up her pointer, walked to the map on the wall and started teaching the European capitals.

'Twas hard to pay attention and at the same time listen for the mine owner to come. Would there be a fight because our teacher turned the Chinese boy away?

When the schoolroom door finally did creak open, Bridgey was writing spelling words on the black-painted boards behind the teacher's desk. She dropped her chalk stone into her dress pocket and turned to stare. Miss Steele saw her stop but forgot to scold, being busy watching the door herself.

Mrs. Maynard came in holding the Chinese boy by his hand. I'd thought her high and mighty when I'd watched her jingle up Main Street in her green gilt sleigh. Close up, though, she seemed more like somebody's mother than a mine owner who could make people jump just by snapping her fingers. "Good afternoon, Miss Steele," she said. "Good afternoon, children. My name is Mrs. Maynard." She didn't need to say who she was. Hadn't the whole camp cheered when they heard she'd bought the Rejoice? Half the camp's miners would have been thrown out of work if she hadn't taken over and kept the gold mine going.

The smallest girls dropped her a curtsy. The rest of us stood up and said all together, "Good afternoon, Ma'am," the way teacher made us when visitors came.

Mrs. Maynard's eyes crinkled at that. She asked, "May I watch awhile, Miss Steele? I have been trying to find time to visit school ever since I moved here."

"Bridget, bring the visitor's seat," Miss Steele ordered. Bridgey pulled a chair away from the wall to set near the teacher's desk. Mrs. Maynard thanked her and sat down, drawing off her long gloves, loosening her wraps.

The Chinese boy stood beside her. If it scared him meeting up with Miss Steele again, his face didn't show it. It hid everything but how different he was from us.

Grinning, Bridgey backed against the wall to watch what would happen. But the quarrel we all expected between Mrs. Maynard and our teacher didn't start. Miss Steele took up her grading book and said, "Fourth reading group to the front when I call out your names: Renny Sholto." I went and stood by the teacher's desk. "Doreen Brodie, Finn Brodie, Kevin Brodie, Rose Dunderdale, Maura McMinn, Hedda Volk, Jules Whangelski." The others lined up beside me, Finn towering above us, him being fourteen.

"This is my largest reading group. They are mainly eleven- and twelve-year-olds," Miss Steele explained.

There was only one copy of McGuffey's Second Reader. We took the numbered paragraphs in turn, stumbling over the words as the primer passed down the row. Finn hadn't much knack for reading. He squinted at the page, not saying anything. After we'd all had a try, Mrs. Maynard put her hand out for the book. She opened it toward the back and gave it to the Chinese boy. "Please read a few paragraphs for the teacher, Zi," she said.

The boy studied the page. I crossed my fingers hoping he'd not shirk it, like Finn, and let kind Mrs. Maynard down. I oughtn't to have worried. None of us ever read better. He made the words sound like a story.

"Perhaps you can see, Miss Steele," Mrs. Maynard said, "why I hope Zi will be able to go to school here in Miner's Chance. In the three years he has lived in

America he has shown unusual talent, perhaps even genius. If he does not continue his schooling, all chance of making something worthwhile of his abilities might be wiped out."

While Miss Steele was making up her answer, Mrs. Maynard said to us, "My parents were missionaries. China was one of the places we lived while I was growing up. I was the first foreign child most people there had ever seen. When I went into the street they gathered around me. They touched my yellow hair to see if it was real. They felt my clothes and skin. When I smiled, they smiled back. I hope the faces of Miner's Chance will smile at Zi as those Chinese faces smiled at me."

Sis Paunce must have whispered something to somebody because Miss Steele said, "Please repeat what you said aloud, Sis, so we all may share it."

Sis shook her head, her face flushing red but when nobody else spoke, finally she had to. "I said, 'They'll never touch him and smile, like she said, because everybody knows Chinese are filthy.'"

Even little Nora could see that didn't fit. "No, Sis" she said, pointing, "see how washed he looks. Like Teacher's white apron."

"Nora, Sis, you will both hold your tongues until given permission to speak," Miss Steele said.

But the kids were too stirred up to stay quiet. "Sis meant filthy like they give people foreign diseases," Cedric Paunce said to back his sister up. "And they get people to smoke opium. Opium turns people crazy."

"My da says they eat cats and dogs," Finn said. "That's why they stink." The Brodie kids all nodded their red heads as if they knew their brother spoke Gospel truth.

The mine owner answered them kindly. "I am sure when you children get to know Zi, you will find you are mistaken." That should have shamed Finn and Cedric and Sis for speaking so rude to a lady. But they just stared at the mine owner, their eyes hard as pebbles.

Miss Steele said to Mrs. Maynard, "They repeat what they hear at home, though more crudely. Their parents would demand my dismissal if I dared admit an Oriental to the school. And, I have no authority to do so."

"I have brought the authority," Mrs. Maynard answered. She laid a paper on the desk. "This is a letter from Dr. Applegate who pays your salary so the children may have schooling. I spoke to him and he is willing to let Zi enter as an experiment."

Miss Steele didn't look sure about that but I think she knew she'd lost. She made one last try to keep the Chinese boy out. "We are overcrowded. Every desk is taken."

"Annie's out sick. Remember, Teacher? Nobody's sitting here." Nora patted the bench beside her.

"Do not be ridiculous. No boy is permitted to sit on the girls' side of the classroom and you know that. Now I have heard the last remark from you, Miss, that I want to hear all day."

Nora hated being put down in front of people. Her

eyes teared up. "Then he can sit with my brother. He can, can't he, Renny?" That Nora. Though I'd put her life in danger, she still trusted me!

Finn glared across the half circle at me. His look said, Say no or I'll make you sorry! The others eyed me, too, except the Chinese boy. Below his fringe of black hair he stared through us like we weren't there.

"Well, what about that, Renny? Would you like sharing your desk with this—this person?" Miss Steele asked.

If I said no she'd have her excuse for not keeping the boy at school. And how my da'd rage if I didn't! He'd already had a lot to say about how wrong 'twas, the new mine owner bringing those heathens into camp. But how could I shut out the poor kid standing there so still? He only wanted what I wanted, what all there who weren't born in America wanted, a chance at being American. So I said, "He can sit with me."

Mrs. Maynard pulled her coat over her shoulders and straightened her hat. "Then it is decided, Zi, that you shall attend school here. Thank you, Miss Steele."

She nodded in my direction. "Thank you, young man."

But things weren't as decided as Mrs. Maynard thought. Finn said, "Chinks don't belong with us."

Cedric said, "You'd never catch me sharing my desk with one."

Sis said, "My papa will come and set all of you straight."

Had those three kept out of it, Miss Steele might have sent the Chinese boy packing as soon as she'd thought up her own reason to. But those Brodies and Paunces were always disputing with her. Things between them had got so bad that whatever they were against, she was for. So she acted like she didn't hear them and waved us back to our desks. The Chinese boy trailed me and inched onto the edge of my bench like he was ready to run.

Mrs. Maynard stood up. "You will enjoy teaching Zi, Miss Steele. His mind is a magnet for information." She got as far as the door and stopped, looking over at the boys' side of the schoolroom. "I want you boys to be kind to Zi," she said, acting for the first time like what she was, a lady rich and powerful enough to order everybody around. The outside door slammed behind her.

Bridgey took the long way back to her desk so she could pass by me and ask, "Why do you always have to save everybody? Da will be furious."

I knew that. I knew, too, why Finn, in the desk ahead of me, was scratching away on his slate. He kept a list in one corner of people he planned to beat up. I didn't have to see it to know he was writing:

> Get Renny
> Get the Chink

3

The Fight

There was one thing we all liked about Friday afternoons. Miss Steele put aside the scolding ways she used to make us pay attention to her teaching and read aloud to us. Sometimes 'twas from the American poets, sometimes a story out of *St. Nicholas* magazine.

But Mrs. Maynard's visit changed that. Our teacher was mad at how things turned out and she let us know it. Though we'd never had it twice in one day before, we got set at arithmetic again. She read a problem to each age group in turn, then another, then another. "And do not let me catch you counting on your fingers," she kept warning.

When the teacher read out a problem, the Chinese boy went to work on it. He didn't know he had to do just the ones for the fourth reading group. I didn't explain, not wanting to get sent back to the punishment stool for talking.

He figured on a little thing with beads he took out of his pocket. It worked like magic. His answers all came right, even those for the oldest group Bridgey was in.

Miss Steele didn't know that. She acted like she didn't see his hand when he held it up to tell his answers.

It seemed hours before she said, "That will be all for today. No, do not run, Finn. Girls, keep your voices down!" I shoved my slate under the desk top and walked to the wall where our coats hung on pegs. Everybody stayed clear away. You'd think sitting by the Chinese boy made me as different as he was.

Miss Steele always stood on the schoolhouse steps till the last kid closed the gate and started down the road into camp. She'd said at the beginning of the year that she wasn't having any fights in her schoolyard. That day, though, she stayed at her desk. She might as well have put up a sign saying she wasn't watching out for Mrs. Maynard's Chinese boy.

Finn bumped people pushing through the door first. The other boys crowded after. None of them looked back, or nodded me to follow.

Nora and Bridgey drew their shawls over their heads. I wound my scarf and pulled on my cap. "Why don't you come on?" Bridgey stamped her boots.

I jerked my head toward the boy. "Finn and the others will be waiting for him where the road gets narrow. I'll see him that far. Maybe I can talk them into going easy on him. You go ahead and take Nora. No need for you to get mixed up in it."

Bridgey frowned. "I'm mixed in it already, being sister to the only boy in school crazy enough to stick up for a Chinaman." She stamped her boots again, that time in anger. "You've heard all Da's said against them being brought here. He'll fume over what you've done. Why do you keep vexing him so?"

"I don't mean to. It just happens."

We'd been whispering, trying to keep others from hearing. But we must have talked louder than we thought because the Chinese boy stepped close and said, "Nobody has to walk with me. I can take care of myself."

"You're going to have to fight," Bridgey said. They were the first words anybody said straight to him. She didn't say them in a kindly way.

He shrugged. "It was the same in California. New boys always had to."

"'Twon't be just because you're new," Bridgey answered, starting to leave, tugging Nora along by her shawl. "If they beat you up too, Renny, maybe you'll think next time."

Nora tried to twist away. "Don't draggle me, Bridgey. I want to walk with Renny and that boy." She couldn't get loose and Bridgey pulled her through the doorway.

"Why are you lingering? You know I do not allow you to dawdle inside after you have been dismissed." Miss Steele stood over me, her coat on and the key to the school in her hand. She shooed me out onto the steps. The Chinese boy came after. Down the road Bridgey and Nora scuffled away. Beyond them the rest of the girls waited at the curve to see the fight.

Miss Steele fastened the door and stamped across the schoolyard. Wong Gum Zi and I followed at a distance.

"Are you any good at fighting?" I asked him. "Boys always have to fight their first day."

"I have had to learn," he said.

Miss Steele started rounding up the girls, herding them down the hill with the rolled black umbrella she carried everywhere. When we reached where they'd been, Finn stepped out of the trees. He always took charge of the First Day fights. "How old is he?" he asked me. The other boys moved up to listen in.

"How should I know?"

"Eleven," Wong Gum Zi said without waiting to be asked.

"He's skinnier than ten," Kevin said.

"Yeah," I said. "Maybe one of the little kids should fight him."

"But he talks old," Jules said, speaking past the boy instead of to him like everybody did in the classroom.

Finn lined us up by size. Him and me and Jules were too tall alongside Wong Gum Zi, and the rest too short. That left Kevin Brodie who looked twice as strong as the boy but was his same height. I tried to point that out but nobody wanted to listen.

Wong Gum Zi took off his coat and jacket, folded them and laid them on a snowbank beside the road. He unbuttoned his sleeves and rolled them up. Then he took a stand like boxers I'd seen pictures of. Everybody laughed, him all angles and so thin a coyote could carry him off. "Looks like a grasshopper," Cedric said. "Step up and smash him, Kevin."

Kevin swaggered up and shot out a fist. Zi leaned out of the way and jigged backward. Kevin sent out his other fist. Zi jigged sideways. Kevin charged. Too sudden to see how it happened, one fist struck Kevin's chest and the other his chin. Kevin's head jerked back and his knees folded. He fell on his back, eyes shut, his face pale green, lip swelling fat and purple while we watched.

"Kevin!" Finn yelled. He dropped down and shook his brother. Kevin didn't rouse. Finn leapt up and jumped on the Chinese boy.

"Wait," I yelled, trying to pull him off. "Be fair." His big fists hurt bad enough when he just fooled around. In a rage they beat like sledgehammers.

Jules grabbed my coat and swung me away and hung on, leaving Finn free to whip Zi. "He'll kill him," I gasped at Jules, cutting a blow to his head that made my knuckles crack and bleed. Cedric rounded up the smaller boys and sent them against me, kicking, pulling, pounding. I wasn't going to fight them. They pulled me down. I fell, striking my head, and lost my wind when they piled on top. I was dying.

"Stop, stop, he's not dead," somebody shouted. They backed off me and I drew a breath so deep it cut like ice in my chest. I thought they meant me but 'twas Kevin they circled round. He sat up shaking his head, his back plastered with snow. Finn eased him to his feet. He wobbled, but he stood blinking and began to cry.

Over to one side Zi tried to stand but he only made it to his knees. One side of his face was puffed up. Blood drained onto the snow from his nose and mouth. "Look what you've done," I said to Finn, "you, twice his size."

"He oughtn't to be in the school. You're to blame, not me." He looked sullen and so did the rest of them. They'd won, but the fight wasn't fair like other times. They moved in a clump down the road, Finn propping Kevin, nobody talking. I'd never felt so alone. Trying to give the boy a chance, I'd turned every friend I had into my enemy.

Once they passed out of sight I started after, thinking that Bridgey was right. I did always try to save everybody. I did take up with people nobody else gave a thought to. It happened without my planning.

A retching sound made me turn. Wong Gum Zi still knelt, throwing up. Too bad for him. I'd done all I was going to. I took a few more steps. 'Twas no good. I couldn't leave him like that. I slogged back through the snow and looked down at him. "Come on. I'll see you home." That's all I will do, though, I promised myself, bracing against the smell of blood and vomit.

"There is a handkerchief in my pocket," he said, "if you could please get it." I found it and held it out. He wrapped snow in it and pressed it to his face.

It took awhile to walk him home. He kept having to rest against trees and once to throw up some more. When we were nearly there he asked if I'd come in and help explain to Mrs. Maynard. We kicked through the snow to the back of her tall, wooden house. He pointed at the door of a building he said she used for her office and I rapped on it. She opened the door and let out a cry, dropping to her knees to put her arms around him. "Who did this, Zi?" He didn't say, though he was sure to know Finn's name.

I said, "New boys always have to fight their first day to show what they're made of. Should they put up a good enough fight then they get left alone, after." At least that's how 'twas up till then. No telling whether the old ways would hold.

"I hoped it would be different here," she said. "Poor child. Can you walk well enough to go ask your father to put some packs on your face? If he thinks you need the doctor, I will send for him." Zi bowed and his nose went to bleeding again. Through his wadded handkerchief he thanked me for standing by him.

When he'd gone off she touched my chin making it feel cool where it hurt the most. "Do you need packs, too?"

"No Ma'am."

"I am grateful to you, Renny Sholto, for taking Zi's part at school. I was afraid no one would." Afraid? Her afraid? I thought when you owned a gold mine you never had to be afraid again. "Would you like some hot milk?"

I shook my head. "I've got to get on now, Ma'am. I work for Mr. McMinn at the livery stable."

"I have a request before you go. Will you walk Zi home from school each day? I will get him there in the mornings."

"Me walking him home won't keep him from getting beat up. I tried to keep them off him today and see what happened."

"I will be glad to pay you to escort him."

I shook my head. "You'd have to send a man to make it work. But that'd just get their dander up and they'd try harder to get at him, riled as they are that he's in the school." It made me uneasy, her talking to me like I was her equal. 'Twas for her to decide, not me.

"He has never had a friend. If you have as much spirit as your little sister, you would make a good one. Could you find it in your heart to befriend him?"

If I'd seen things as my da saw them, I'd have said no right out. Everybody was already against me. But thinking over what she asked I found myself saying, "I'll try."

Before she made too much of that I added, "Having me along though, won't keep their fists off him."

"Let us take it day by day and hope for the best. Tell me. Was the tall girl at the blackboard your sister, too?"

"Yes, Ma'am. Her name's Bridget."

"You and Nora look remarkably like her."

"That's what everybody says, us all having our da's looks."

"Zi and I are fortunate to know you. I am certain things will go better from now on with you on his side," she said before closing her door.

I wished I felt as sure about that as she seemed to.

4

Da Makes a Grim Promise

I'd hardly got inside our cabin after work before Mam was asking, "What is this tale Nora's been telling of a Chinaman in the school?" As I was explaining, in came Bridgey from helping at the boardinghouse and let slip that the new boy shared my desk.

"Why ever did you let the teacher put him in with you?" Mam asked, her cheeks flushed with worry. "No telling what your da will say."

"You'd have done the same, Mam," I said. "You always stick up for people when somebody takes against them. And you'd like him. He's quick to learn and plucky. Though small, he fought Finn like a bobcat."

"Finn fought that skinny little kid?" Bridgey asked. When I nodded, she tossed her head. "Just like him," she said. She'd always found fault with Finn.

Nora said, "I like that Zi. I'm going to ask him to come play."

"No you are not, dearie," Mam said. "There's enough trouble afoot without that." She turned to me. "You're maybe right about him, son. But he's not my worry. You are. You see people's needs too clear. You'll get your heart broke if you don't toughen up."

"Or your backside. By Da," Bridgey said. Mam frowned at Bridgey. She'd frowned a lot that winter, trying to make my big sister start acting grown-up now she'd turned fourteen.

Nora said, "Finn and Cedric and Sis sassed that Mrs. Maynard. You'd soap my tongue did I talk so to a lady."

Mam turned to me, "See? That's why the boy means trouble. Him and his da in camp so short a time and already setting people against each other. 'Tis no wonder gold miners across the state are working to shut them from the camps." We ate arguing. Our shadows bobbed and battled on the log walls.

Afterwards, around eight, Mam said to me, "Go to the Green Eyes and get your da. If he hasn't heard what you've done, we'll hold the news till the morning."

Bridgey put on a bored look when Mam added, "Open your eyes to the good things you see on Main Street, son. Blind them to the bad." She said that same thing every Friday night thinking to shield me from the camp's evils. Even daytimes, with things quieter than at night, she made us cross the street lest we see what went on behind the big windows of the Gilded Lily dance hall. We had to cross again before the billiard parlor and Gambler Jim's place and every one of the saloons. Bridgey said it must dizzy people, watching us Sholto kids steer clear of sinful places.

When I'd got on my coat Mam handed me her pot

lids to clang together in case of bears. "Nobody's reported any yet," she said, "but you could be the first to meet one, now that April's come. And them extra hungry after denning all winter! Leave the lids under the thimbleberry bush where the path ends. Don't forget them on your way back."

"What's the matter with you?" Bridgey asked Nora. Nora was red in the face and kind of swelled up. She had her hand over her mouth.

'Twas clear she was struggling to keep the secret about the bears from leaping out of her mouth. I patted her back and said, "Go ahead and cough if you have to." She made a great coughing that sounded so fake I thought Mam and Bridgey were sure to notice but they didn't.

'Twas good to have Mam's pot lids when I stepped outside. Every shadow the blue moon made on the blue snow looked like a wild animal crouched and waiting. At least, I said aloud to hearten myself, in this gulch we're too poor to dump left-over food outside. That's what brings bears among the houses.

Through the trees ahead I heard the thump of a freighter passing. A horse neighed. Another answered. When I got where I could look up Main Street, crowds were parading the boardwalks. A stagecoach blocked the roadway, the coach dog snarling the camp dogs away from its wheels. Carriages, horses, and wagons piled up in both directions, waiting to get past.

On the balcony outside the Gilded Lily a line of girls kicked and whirled to the tinkle of a piano, lace flashing along the edges of their pink petticoats. They'd be at the top of Mam's list of bad things I was supposed to blind my eyes to, with their sleeveless, low-cut dresses and disorderly behavior. But I knew Bridgey'd beg till I told her all about them. So I stood awhile in the street with the watching miners.

"Throw it. Throw it," the men chanted. A girl slid off her garter and tossed it. It hung overhead, then dropped close, a crinkled blue circle. I swooped it into my pocket to take to Bridgey.

"Give it here, kid. 'Tis no good to you. You can't claim the free dance from her." The men held their hands out but I shoved through them and ran.

Night was my favorite time in camp. With the street so busy, it didn't make sense to zig-zag avoiding sinful places. I felt part of it all and tipped my cap to people who looked like they rated respect. I'd just tipped it to Dr. Applegate outside the billiard parlor when the wide doors swung open and a miner came out. Behind him Finn stood watching a game. He caught sight of me, dropped his shoeshine kit, and pushed forward. I darted into the dark between the Mercantile House and the Miner's Supply. He charged along the boardwalk, shouts of anger raised against his shoving.

Soon he came back peering between the buildings but didn't spy me crouched in the dark. When he'd gone I dodged the street traffic to the other side and ran along the boardwalk, watching my feet. It wouldn't be much of a escape should I break a leg in the gap where one stretch of boards left off and the next began.

They were singing inside the Green Eyes saloon, Da's bass voice shoring up the others. Outside a crowd stood to listen. I searched through it lest Finn be there. But the one person I knew was our priest, Father Fergus, talking to a one-armed beggar.

The clock on the newspaper office bonged eight thirty, Da's curfew time, and I stepped to swing open the saloon doors. Finn leapt from the shadows. He seized my shoulders and slammed me backward. "That's for Kevin getting knocked out and being made to cry. He never cries." He raised me and slammed me down again. "That's for letting the Chink sit in your desk." By that time I'd got my wits back. I bit and kicked to keep my head from being smashed through the boardwalk. Rolling away, I tried to rise to my feet but Finn dragged me by the collar into the saloon. "This here kid of yours is traitor to the school," he said, dropping me at my da's feet.

Mr. Brodie grabbed Finn by the arm. "You say 'Sir' speaking to Mr. Sholto, him who every miner looks up to."

"Sir," Finn said, swallowing like his da had slapped him.

The singing petered out. Da told Finn to climb on the bar. He waved me up there, too. I wished he'd hold me close like he used to when I got hurt. Or smile that special smile of his that always set things right with people. He didn't. He flipped us each a beer rag to wipe our scrapes and asked me, "What makes Finn say you're traitor to the school?" like he was a judge in a court of law and me some criminal.

The saloon was the wrong place to tell about Wong Gum Zi, everybody listening in. But Da waited, looking vexed at the commotion us kids caused. Nobody else in the saloon moved, either. They waited, like him, to weigh my answer.

"The new lady that owns the Rejoice, came to school. She brought her houseboy so he could get some learning."

"You mean that Chink kid?" somebody in the crowd asked. I nodded and there came a low whistle. "She looks to have him go to school with you others?" When I nodded again they said, "She's got gall."

"Worse than gall, thinking to do a man's job running a gold mine by herself," Da said.

Mr. Brodie said, "Next she'll be putting her name up to get herself elected mayor." There came a shout of laughter.

"Go on. What else?" Da asked when it got quiet.

"She showed a paper from the doctor so the teacher had to let the boy in. But there wasn't a desk."

Finn said, "So Renny says the Chink can sit with him. I'd not sit with no Chink though the lady begged and begged."

"He's right!" several men said.

"But you will?" Da asked me, frowning. "Why in the name of mischief?"

I didn't dare come out with the truth, that I'd felt

sorry for Zi having nobody to take his part. 'Twould shame Da before the others. They bragged of their hard-heartedness and left feeling sorry for their women. "She said she'd pay me did I walk him home each day and try to keep him from getting beat up," I said. They'd understand if there was money in it.

The priest had come in for his nightly pint and sat listening. "'Tis naught but a kids' quarrel, Lon," he said. "Why grill him so?"

"You don't understand, Father," my da answered, "no more than my boy does. 'Tis far more than a kids' quarrel he's got hisself mixed in. There he sits in trouble up to his neck and hasn't the sense to know it."

"How so?" asked the priest.

"Those Chinamen. So feared are they in the gold camps that over in Leadville, miners blew up a cabin with one in it. Now they've come here. They should be got rid of, not made welcome the way Renny's done like they were President Garfield hisself."

"But they are house servants. They don't threaten your jobs," Father Fergus said.

"Should they be let stay, this town will get the name of a safe place of their kind. Others will come, miners, who'll work for less pay than us, with our families, can get by on. Old Paunce'd be pleased as punch to hire them at the Kitkat and leave us go. Wasn't he only yesterday talking to that Denver man about cheap labor?"

Mr. Brodie broke in, talking at Finn, "What's this got to do with you?" Finn never was much with words. He couldn't seem to say why he'd got so mad. He just sat turning his cap in his hands. Mr. Brodie told him, "You're way bigger than Renny. Quit picking on him. You boys shake hands."

Finn didn't move. Mr. Brodie raised his fist. Finn wriggled along the bar. He crushed my hand. I grit my teeth to keep from flinching. "You never said she was paying."

"You gave me no chance."

"I'll take that money," he whispered low.

"I haven't got it yet," I whispered back.

"When you do."

"What do I get out of it, then?"

"I'll leave him be."

"You're only part of it. Should Kevin or Jules or any other hurt him I'd not get paid." It wasn't the time to say the money wasn't a sure thing. Maybe I could get some for him, maybe I couldn't.

"I can hold them off him. How about it?"

"I guess."

He let go my hand. "Why side with that Chink anyhow? He's dirt." I shrugged, tired of explaining.

Da called to me, "Come on. Time we got home."

"'Tis not near time, Lon," Mr. Brodie said.

"Just one more drink and one more song," another man coaxed. Da smiled at them and put on his jacket and we left. He led the Kitkat miners but when Mam sent for him, home he went.

He stalked across the street. A man had set up

business on the boardwalk in front of the newspaper office. He'd put low barrels to sit on and nailed up a sign,–NIGHT DENTISTRY—SIX P.M. TO MORNING—TEETH PULLED—PAINLESS. Da asked him could we use his barrels for a bit and we sat down.

"All right," Da said. "You've been called a traitor to the school before the whole saloon. There'll be many there who deem you a traitor to the miners, too. You said you did it for money. Knowing you, I doubt 'twas that. What made you act such a tomfool?"

"There was this kid, like I said. Everybody took against him. It didn't seem fair, nobody speaking up for him. So I did."

"He had that rich lady speaking for him. Why'd you have to horn in?"

"Because if one of us kids didn't give him a place to sit the teacher'd throw him out."

"What need has he for learning anyway, just to run errands and keep the mine owner's house?" Da asked.

Mrs. Maynard said he needed a education to keep from wasting his brain. Da wouldn't want to hear that so I said, "Maybe like the rest of us. To pass the time till we get hired for the mine."

"You're as bad as Finn," he said shaking his head back and forth like I was some freak. "He thinks, if he does at all, with his fists. You think with your heart and leave your head out of it. I'm not surprised you've got yourself in this mess, everybody against you."

"But, Da . . ."

"Don't 'but Da' me. Though that lady offered you all the gold in her mine you shouldn't have said you'd do as she asked. You tell her your da said you're to have no more to do with him."

"Though I promised?"

He swore then and cuffed me about the ears. But he'd preached to us kids so often that promises are made to be kept, he couldn't ask me to go back on mine. "Why'd you promise?"

"It seemed right."

"It wasn't right. But you've made your promise. Now I'll make one. If any other Chinks follow those others here, I'll blow up their cabins. It'll just be luck if they aren't inside." He strode away down the boardwalk leaving me to run after.

He spoke only once again. "You shamed me tonight, letting Finn drag you in off the street."

"Da," I wailed, "he's way bigger."

"He'd not have dragged me when I was your age. Size doesn't decide who wins, grit does." He marched off, his long steps leaving me to scrabble under the bush for the pan lids and hurry home alone amid the moon's crouching shadows.

When I'd bade Mam goodnight—Da kept his back to me—I climbed to the loft where we kids slept. Like every Friday night, Bridgey waited to hear what I'd seen on Main Street. I dropped the silk garter on the rough coverlet of her bed. She pounced like I'd brought home treasure. I told about the dancing girls and a fight I'd passed and mine with Finn. "Is that all?" she asked as though she'd expected a murder at least or a fire or something really scary. I started naming the good things Mam said to look for. Bridgey began to yawn.

"Did Da know about you and that Wong Gum Zi?" she asked. I nodded but didn't tell her what he'd said.

'Twas too awful to repeat.

5

The White Raven

Before Da left for the Kitkat Saturday morning, he piled me with work enough to last till Tuesday. Besides my regular chores he said to get the pack rats out of the cabin and the heavy April snow off the roof. I was also to do the same for old Miss Hettie who lived up the hill. "Wet as these last snows have been, their weight could flatten her cabin," he said. "And don't you go near the Maynard place."

Mam was peeling potatoes for Sunday's stew while she coached Bridgey and Nora in lacemaking. When I'd chopped wood enough to hold us till Monday, carried out ashes and brought in water, she pointed to a bulge in the canvas she'd nailed up for a ceiling. "I'm glad he asked you to get rid of those rats," she said. "I can't stand them running back and forth up there above my cooking pots."

I stacked the wooden crates we used for chairs and climbed up. One slash with a stick turned the rat's nest over. Babies tumbled out and scattered squeaking across the canvas and up the walls into the roof. One missed its footing and fell over the edge of the canvas, landing near the girls. They jumped up screaming, their lace pillows held high over their heads. I tossed the nest in the stove, then cornered the rat and threw it outside.

Mam hardly got the girls quiet when a knock came at the door. Nora opened it and gave another screech. "He came to play. He didn't wait till I asked him." There stood Wong Gum Zi with his face bruised from yesterday's battering. A white bird rode on his shoulder. Behind him was his da. "Come in quick," Nora said, holding the door wide. In they came, Mr. Wong dressed again in the yellow robe that marked this as a special occasion.

It unsettled things, Nora asking them in. Mam, speechless at her house filling up with Chinese, wrung her hands. Bridgey bent over her pillow and didn't look up. That left it to me, what to do, me wondering if Da, deep in the mine, could feel that enemies were in his cabin. I stammered, "Tell your da this here is my mam. You know Bridgey and Nora." Zi spoke to his da.

Mr. Wong bowed to each in turn. Zi did, too, and then said, "Let me introduce my father, Mr. Wong Gum, and my bird, White Star."

Their fine manners impressed Mam. She dropped a curtsy and signaled the girls to do the same. Bridgey stood up and did as Mam wanted though she wasn't over her fluster enough to look Zi and his da in the eye.

Mr. Wong spoke and handed Mam something rolled up. Zi relayed what his da wanted said. "We have come to express my father's thanks that your son stood by me yesterday and has agreed to befriend me." His face almost creased in a smile, but he didn't go quite that far. I guessed their visit was meant to be serious.

Nora danced around, clapping her hands. She pulled Zi's sleeve. "Come see my solid gold rocks," she said soft, not to interrupt too much.

"Leave him be, Nora," I said. "He's come on business. Not to play."

Mam unwound the roll Mr. Wong brought. 'Twas a blue cloth. Hundreds of threads sewed across it made a picture of a mountain stream with two people kneeling by. The way Mam ran her fingers across the stitches I could tell she thought it beautiful. "Do I talk with the boy to thank the man?" she asked me like Zi was stone deaf.

Before I could speak, the white bird did. It said, "Hello, lady," then flew over near Bridgey. "Hello, lady," it said again. Mam and Bridgey were surprised into smiles.

"Who'd believe it, a bird speaking words?" Mam asked. She looked pleased but worried, too, lest it be wrong, being so strange. Something, maybe Mr. Wong standing silent, made her remember his gift. She said to Zi, "This handwork is too fine for our rough cabin. Thank your da for me but tell him I can't take it."

Zi told his da what Mam said. Mr. Wong shook his head and held up his hands, speaking low. "He says, it is not nearly enough to thank for Renny's bravery," Zi said.

"Bravery?" Bridgey whispered behind me. "Stupidness!" But then seeing Mam didn't know what to answer she said, "Give him a piece of your lace in return."

"That's it," Mam said. "Find him one. I'll pour him a cup of coffee." I showed Mr. Wong to our one chair and took down my piled boxes so we could all sit. Bridgey brought a lace doily and handed it to Mr. Wong. He rose and bowed to her and sat again, spreading the piece across his knee to study the design. She pulled her box over near him and went to work with her bobbins, crossing and twisting the threads so he'd see how lace is made. When Bridgey acted nice she was worth two of the rest of us.

"Where did you get that bird?" I asked Zi.

"I found her back home in China. She fell from her nest. Or perhaps the ravens thrust her out because she is an albino. My father says birds either worship their albinos or peck them to death." The raven had settled on the edge of the table with a rustle of white feathers. It looked at one and then another as each spoke.

Mam handed Mr. Wong a cup of coffee. When he saw he was the only one served, he nodded his thanks but didn't drink. She poured herself a cup, then, and came and sat down, too kind to be rude to company no matter who they were. "Don't we get any?" Bridgey asked.

"Of course you do," Mam said. "I don't know what I'm doing today. Pour everyone some." Mr. Wong looked more at home once Mam sat down and started drinking, too.

"Does your bird fly loose?" she asked Zi. She still wore that troubled look like she didn't know if what was going on in her house ought to be going on.

"I do not dare take that risk. Her nest is in a cage behind the carriage house where we stay. Sometimes a raven flock settles down on the cage like a black cloud. I do not know whether they are inviting her to fly with them or seeking to do her harm."

Nora brought her iron pyrite rocks and piled them beside Zi. "Every single one of them is solid gold," she said smiling up at him. He smiled back and weighed one on his hand, not making fun that she thought them real.

After the Chinese left Mam said, "I fear what your da's going to say, me treating them like company."

"We couldn't just stand staring at each other," Bridgey said. She tacked the silk picture above the table.

"Best hide it away," I said.

She wouldn't listen. "See how the silver threads catch the light," she kept saying. "I bet nobody else has one so fine."

Da exploded when he saw it and heard who brought it. "What if a miner's wife had come calling while they lingered here, or a lady, to buy lace? They'd have caught you swapping gifts like you and those Chinamen were old friends," he said to Mam, tearing the picture down. "You're all as bad as Renny. You bar that door against them should they come here again."

"You'd not want me acting less polite than a China-man," Mam said. Da just gave a disgusted grunt and she went on, "The Good Book says to welcome all comers lest amongst them be angels in disguise." Holding the ripped picture against her, her color high, she looked like a Irish queen.

Da snorted. "Peg," he said in that same testy voice he used to explain things when Nora didn't understand, "the Bible wasn't talking about Chinese."

Mam snapped, "How do you know?" huffy as Nora when Da talked down to her. She rattled pans on the stove too loud to hear Da's answer. Then she turned and said, "I don't know what's come over me. 'Tis like I said before. Bringing in those people is making the camp choose up sides. Even us. Even here."

Da said, "Yes, and should they manage to stay on, they'll end up driving us Irish out."

"Not Zi," Nora said, stamping her foot, "not his da." But his words struck the rest of us silent like a bell tolled for the dead.

Most families in Miner's Chance went to church Sunday mornings, though most unmarried men didn't bother. We Catholics worshipped at the Gilded Lily. Everybody else had church upstairs above the Spiffy Gent Saloon when one of their circuit-riding preachers came. Gambling and drinking kept on at the saloon while hymns and sermons rang out above. But the Gilded Lily didn't open for dancing till Mass finished, the manager and a lot of the girls being Catholics themselves.

That Sunday blew in bright and cold. A sharp wind whipped aside the yellow cloud from the smelter and as we hurried down Main Street we could see the mountaintops rimming our canyon. Blowing snow made them look like they were smoking.

Mam and the girls kept themselves warm gossiping about everybody they saw. When Mrs. Maynard passed up the other side headed for the Spiffy Gent, Bridgey said, "See her, not dressed much better than the rest of us. People say money's wasted on her when she uses none of it for show."

Da kept warm lecturing me. "I don't know where you came by your love for the underdog," said he. "But you've no need to go looking for outsiders to spend it on. The Irish miner is the underdog in this camp, sure enough. Them in the big houses count us fit only for ridicule and digging. That's why we need to hang together. Fighting amongst ourselves opens us to attack."

The Paunces came out of their stone house about then and took his mind off berating me. "There they come for their once a year Mass," he growled. "They only show up when the bishop's here to give our church some class."

The worn wagon the bishop used when he traveled from camp to camp slouched in front of the dance hall. In honor of his coming, the ladies borrowed potted palms from the hotel and somebody lent their vase of wax roses. A white shawl veiled the dry-goods boxes set on end for the altar.

Ever since he'd come to our camp Father Fergus had been wanting a real church to say Mass in. He didn't like it that sometimes the undertaker kept corpses cool in the room where we met. Or that we could hear his homily only if he yelled when the blacksmith next door went to hammering on his anvil.

I guess he'd told his troubles to the bishop because the old man gave a long homily on respect being paid to the Lord. He made it plain that worshipping in a dance hall wasn't his idea of how to be respectful.

It seemed to me he preached over the miner's heads right at Mr. Paunce, the only one there with enough money to buy bricks or timber to build a church. Mr. Paunce must have thought so, too. He spoke out at the end of Mass, "I will pay for a fine stone church if it is called St. Maeve's, to honor my wife and daughter who bear that name."

I could tell by the way the miners whispered that there was something bold-faced about Mr. Paunce's offer. Father Fergus whispered too, to the old bishop. At last the bishop asked, "How much are you offering to the Lord, sir?" Mr. Paunce named his price.

The bishop said, "Thank you for that sum. I accept it. But I will expend it according to the needs of this parish. One third of it will build a usable log chapel. Two thirds I will turn over to Father Fergus for his work among the poor and sick. The chapel will be more aptly named St. John's."

Afterwards the Paunces led the bishop away to feed

him dinner at their house. Their long faces showed the meal wasn't going to be the celebration they'd expected. The rest of us stood around in the street swinging our arms to keep warm, the grownups having their weekly chat, us kids listening in. The women had a lot to say about Mr. Paunce thinking to get a church named for his missus and Sis.

After a time Da and the men drifted off to practice for the fire brigade he'd got organized. Sunday afternoons they raced through camp drawing the pumper truck, putting out make-believe fires. The townsfolk who'd raised money to buy the truck raised cheers when they passed.

They'd asked Finn, grown so tall and strong, to join the brigade. Walking away he bumped into Bridgey, making sure she saw he was counted one of the men. Bridgey made no sign she'd seen him.

"What's the matter with you?" Mam asked. "'Tis high time you started noticing the boys. Especially him, handsome and red-haired as St. Michael hisself." Bridgey just rolled her eyes. Maybe she wasn't up to arguing so soon after Mass.

Later that afternoon I slipped off to face Mrs. Maynard about the money. Mr. Wong let me in. It being Sunday, she sat reading her Bible close to the parlor grate. The room had green velvet curtains with bobbles around the edges and pictures in carved frames and painted dishes in a corner cabinet. And books. Books to the ceiling like they were there to keep the walls from caving in. Everything seemed to shout, "You don't belong here, miner's boy, in your rough clothes and home-knit stockings sagging down over your boots."

Mrs. Maynard looked up with a smile. Then she turned serious. "Why do you look more battered every time I see you, Renny?"

"Things keep happening," I said, not wanting to talk about it. I explained how Finn would leave off fighting Zi should he get paid.

"That is a relief," she said. "I was beginning to regret asking you to befriend Zi, it seemed to expose you to such harm. Do you think two cents a week will make him keep his fists to himself?"

"Maybe. You never know with Finn."

"You offer him that much. If that does not satisfy him, send him to me." She said something to Mr. Wong. He brought her reticule. She took some coins from it and dropped them in my hand. It didn't seem right, her having to pay me just so I could pay Finn. I said as much.

"Perhaps I can persuade you to take some for yourself."

"Maybe sometime," I said.

But not knowing how much to ask for, I didn't ask for any.

6

A Daring Theft

Before school on Monday I paid Finn. "Remember, that's to keep your fists off Mrs. Maynard's Chinese boy," I told him. He gave me that wide grin of his leaving me to guess if he'd do what he'd said.

Miss Steele had set the classroom up to show how she felt, having to take a Oriental into her school. She'd pushed the desks near to hers, all but mine. Mine, with Wong Gum Zi in it, stood in back next to the punishment stool like we might give the other kids the smallpox. That corner being farthest from the stove was cold as creek ice. Frost glinted along the logs.

Again that day teacher acted like she didn't see Zi when he put up his hand. So she didn't know he parsed the grammar sentences right or did his dictation exercise perfect. He worked faster than most. In the time left over, he wrote with a gold pencil in a little notebook he kept on his lap. Sitting so close, I couldn't help seeing:

> White Star stirs my memories of China.
> When she sits on my shoulder
> and babbles Chinese in my ear, I see

our village again and hear its familiar
clatter around me.

another time he wrote:

Our teacher has her back to the class.
Standing there she reminds me of my
mother. They both coil their hair,
like black silk, into the same knot
along their necks. Where light touches,
there is a flash of blue.
How kindly my mother looked at me, always, and
how gentle her hands were. But when
Miss Steele turns there is anger in
her eyes.

The kids showed how they felt about having to go to
school with the Chinese boy by teasing. They made
lunchtime and recess a torment, buzzing around Zi's
ears like hornets. Sis started it. "Would you like a lemon
pastry, China boy?" she asked. Before he could answer,
she mashed it in his hair.

After school I walked him down the road to camp.
Most of the others followed us, taunting. Sis shouted
loudest, "You'll give Renny the Chinese rot." When
Finn threw stones, Sis called out, "Watch the yellow cur
run with his tail between his legs."

Not that Zi ran. He didn't pay any more attention
than if the taunts were snowflakes that melted before
they landed on him. "'Tis lucky Finn is such a good
shot," I said.

"How can you say he is a good shot?" he asked. "He has thrown stones all the way down the hill and has not hit us once."

"He'd hit us every time, weren't he getting paid. Lots of times I've seen him sail a rock across Main Street and kill a rat on the run."

Zi smiled. "You've outwitted him, the one I fear the most. Thank you."

Even the little ones teased. The five-year-old Brodie twins ran beside us pushing at the corners of their eyes to make them slant. Mab giggled and Mayo shouted, "Piggytailed Chinaman, oink, oink, oink." Zi took their hands and ran with them down the road, oinking too. Which set all the Brodies hollering at the twins.

So it went. Every day in school and after, the kids kept up their teasing. I think it troubled me more than it did Zi, though Finn only let a rock hit me now and then to remind me how good he was at keeping his promise.

The trouble Da said to expect from the camp people didn't turn out to be much. One miner grabbed me by the coat front to scold when he saw me with Zi, another splashed us with a blast of tobacco juice. But that was all. The big change Zi made in my life was that Mr. McMinn started giving me boxing lessons, Da having told him I needed some. "Having took up with that Chinaman, he'll need to know how to fight, to protect hisself," is what he said to the stable master. That made it sound like the lessons were for my own good. I thought they were so I'd not shame him again, getting bested in a fight.

"I already know how to fight, Da," I told him. "I'm good at it. But I don't like hurting people."

"McMinn will teach you to like it and teach you some boldness and trickery at the same time. Maybe learning fisticuffs, you'll learn to stand up for yourself."

I hated the lessons. I went home aching from them every day. The stable master seemed to enjoy punching at me while the end of his cigar glowed and dimmed. I suspicioned it was his way of paying me out for being friends with Zi.

It's funny. Sometimes the hardest times turn into the best times. The spring of 1881 was like that for me. Da chafed at everything I did. Mr. McMinn kept battering me. The boys I'd always been pals with made it clear I was their enemy. Yet a friendship started up between me and Wong Gum Zi like none I'd had before. And though most everybody was set on stamping it out, it kept growing.

It started with him asking wasn't there some way he could show his thanks for me taking his side. I asked could he teach me to use the magic thing with beads he solved problems with. He said 'twas a abacus and 'twasn't magic. We went into the outdoor kitchen behind Mrs. Maynard's house. He showed me how the abacus worked, with its rods for tens, hundreds, thousands. Mr. Wong watched and fed us food and problems. For the first time I saw arithmetic might make some sense. I'd never noticed before there were patterns to it.

In the days after that we took to reading books. Mrs. Maynard let us use what we wanted off her shelves so long as we were careful. And we taught each other our games. It was hard for him to get the hang of my knife as he learned mumblety-peg. I had as hard a time not pressing too hard with his paintbrushes. The time after school before I had to be at the livery stable became the best part of my day. That was a secret I kept to myself.

One afternoon Finn followed us in at Mrs. Maynard's gate. "Where do you think you're going?" I asked him.

"I want to talk to the Chink," Finn said. "'Tis none of your business to ask why."

"Please stay until he leaves," Zi whispered .

Finn idled around . When he saw there was no hope I'd let him talk to Zi without me hearing he said, "Hey, kid. Nora said you got a talking crow. I'll pay you some money I'm getting right along if you sell it to me." He stirred his hand around in his pocket. Coins clinked. Even counting his shoeshine money, there couldn't be many. I'd only paid him twice.

"'Tis not a crow," I said. "That's how much you know."

"Whatever 'tis I want it."

"Thank you for offering," Zi said, being a lot more polite than me. "However, I shall never sell her. She means more to me than money. But you may see her if you like."

"Why not bring Star out?" I asked. It wasn't smart to

let Finn know where the bird was kept.

Zi ran behind the house and came back in a while with the raven. "Hello Renny," White Star said.

"Make it say 'Hello Bridgey'," Finn said.

"Whatever for?" I asked him.

"'Tis for her I want the bird. Maybe then she'll pay me some mind." He said to Zi, "Make it say what I asked. And make it tell me hello."

Zi spoke softly, stroking her feathers. Star just pecked away at Zi's fingers. Zi said some more things but Star stayed silent.

"Dumb bird!" Finn said.

"Bad boy!" White Star said. I shouldn't have laughed. Finn snatched at the raven. She rapped his knuckles with her heavy beak and flew up to perch on a branch.

Finn sucked his fingers and told Zi, "You've no call to make her sass me." He grabbed a stone off the rock garden and threw it. Star squawked and flapped to a windowsill, one tail feather dragging down. Finn slung another stone that sped straight though I threw myself against him. It struck the bird, splintering the window. Star flew crookedly over the roof calling, "Bad, bad, bad, bad."

Zi covered his face with his arms. The crash of glass brought Mr. Wong from the kitchen and Mrs. Maynard out of her office. Finn ran away calling, "Look, I tried to buy her decent and you wouldn't."

Day was sliding toward dark. A light went on in the Paunces' glassed-in garden room next door making fern patterns on the snow around us. 'Twas time I got to the livery stable but being with Zi seemed more important than the whomping Mr. McMinn was sure to give me for not showing up. Mrs. Maynard and Mr. Wong set off in different directions calling. I sat on the steps to the carriage house with Zi. He was too broken up to be of any help hunting.

He talked and talked of White Star. How he'd first found her. How he was told to leave her behind in China but hid her under his coat when he and his da boarded the boat to America. Only Star gave him hope that he'd live through the voyage when the passengers sickened and some died in the dirty, crowded, leaking ship. And how Star not being discovered when at last the boat docked, seemed like a promise that they'd get to stay in America. Mr. Wong and Mrs. Maynard returned while he was still talking. Neither one had found even a feather.

I searched our gulch after supper. White Star wasn't shut in the Brodies' outhouse or held captive under the pails by their back door. The Brodies' cabin, like any holding thirteen kids, shook the house with shouts and bickering. I couldn't believe the white bird still had breath or feathers if she was inside.

Next morning when the Kitkat whistle called the miners to work, I sprawled on my pallet faking sleep. Another day with Da saying how grateful I ought to be that Mr. McMinn was toughening me and everybody at school teasing, wasn't worth rising up for. And Zi, should he come to school, would likely cry all day over his lost bird.

Nora put her ice-cold hand on my face. "You'll be late for school, Ren. You'll get sent to the punishment stool again." Still I didn't get up.

She must have told I wasn't coming because Mam raised her voice. "Renny, get down here in a hurry, or go without food till supper." That got me moving. I ate my porridge slowly and left home late, too downhearted to zig-zag back and forth across Main Street.

Just before I passed the sawmill, a burro train left it and started up toward the Rejoice. Usually I'd race to take the school road before they did. But I stepped to the side and let them go ahead. They'd make a good excuse for me being late did Miss Steele scold me too hard.

The rattle of the timbers the burros carried startled the raven flock out of the pine trees. I looked for White Star among them. She wasn't there. Did they drive her off? Did they peck her to death? I wondered.

When I walked into school I stood by the coat pegs waiting for Miss Steele to say, "Get your slate and write 'I will not be late' until I tell you to stop." She didn't say it. She said, "Sit down and get to work," with a secret kind of smile as if she knew something amazing. The kids looked at me like they were bursting with news to tell, and thank goodness, here came somebody who hadn't heard it yet.

Zi sat there smiling. When I slid in beside him he

looked straight ahead but whispered , "Star came home." I took up my slate and wrote, "Is she hurt?" Before he wrote back I knew she wasn't, the way he kept beaming.

There was a breathless feel about school that morning. Everybody seemed to shoot off sparks. "What's got them wrought up?" I wrote.

Below the sentence he was parsing he answered, "An emerald brooch." And later, "With diamonds."

"What about it?"

"Someone stole it."

"Whose was it?"

"Mrs. Paunce's."

When lunchtime came and we could talk, I climbed with Zi in the lower branches of the schoolyard pine. I wanted to hear about White Star away from the shoving, teasing kids. But we didn't get let alone. They came pushing below us, heads tipped back, all talking about Mrs. Paunce's fancy pin. Sis elbowed the others and said, "I should be the one to tell Renny. It happened at my house."

She stood under the tree talking about the jewel. Her mam laid it away after she'd paid afternoon calls. She only missed it when she looked for it that morning. "It's the one that she wears for best. There's an emerald the size of a coat button and seventeen diamonds."

"Solid diamonds?" Nora asked. "A solid emerald?"

"What do you mean, solid?" Sis asked her.

"She means real," Bridgey said.

"Of course they were real, you little silly. Mama doesn't wear jewels that aren't and Papa wouldn't rage so over losing a fake. Whoever stole it walked right into our house with dinner guests there and servants everywhere. They climbed to Mama's bedroom and helped themselves from her jewelry box though she always locks it. Then they sneaked down again and out. And nobody saw or heard a thing!"

I shivered at the daring of it. Miner's Chance had holdups on the street, sometimes, and a holdup was tried at the bank at least once a month. The stagecoach was always in danger of being robbed when the gold went to Denver. But upstairs in somebody's bedroom with the house full of people? A slick, second-story burglar must have come to our camp.

That afternoon Mr. Paunce burst in on the school. As Sis had promised, he'd come to set everyone straight about Zi going to school with his kids. He flung open the door and stomped into the schoolroom before Miss Steele could pin up her loose hair.

He didn't greet us the way Mrs. Maynard had. The little girls got up to curtsy but sank back on their bench when he marched right past. He stood at the teacher's desk talking loud. "That Chinese kid's got to go." He scorched Zi with a look. "Mrs. Maynard has no right forcing him on the camp or the school. I want him out of here." He stepped back facing the class, waiting for his orders to be carried out. Nora and the other little ones sat stock-still with fear of him, their eyes starey and noses twitching like rabbits afraid of a fox.

Shouting orders like he was at the Kitkat didn't work with Miss Steele. Maybe she'd have done what he asked had he acted more polite or hadn't she had to stand up to his kids so often. But she wasn't letting a Paunce run her school no matter how old or powerful he was. "I did not want him enrolled," she said. "If you want him expelled you will have to decide the matter with Mrs. Maynard and the doctor. They are the ones who insisted he be here."

For a minute he brushed his beard with the backs of his fingers and looked stumped. Then he said to Sis and Cedric, " Get your coats. You're going home."

"No Papa," Sis shrieked. "There's nothing to do at home."

"You can help your mother. Go on, get your coat."

"Help her do what? All she does is sit. How can I help her sit?" Nora's laugh bubbled out. The other little ones laughed with her. Mr. Paunce stepped over and lifted Sis out of her desk and pushed toward the coat wall. Cedric got up and followed. They put on their wraps and their da shooed them ahead of him from the room. The outside door slammed.

That set me worrying about Zi. Was there any use his trying to learn to be American with so many Americans against him?

7

A Bad Day for Zi (and Nora)

One day during arithmetic we were all quiet for once. Suddenly Miss Steele stood up, her head turned to listen. "What is that clicking noise?"

Zi was figuring on his abacus. It clicked as the beads shot up and down on their little rods. Miss Steele stalked toward us and snatched it from him. "What is this?"

"My abacus, Ma'am."

"What are you doing with it?"

"I am figuring my arithmetic problems."

"You cheat."

Zi looked at her, then at me, then back at her. 'Twas clear he didn't know what she meant. "It is for counting. All Chinese use them."

"Americans do not. American children are not even allowed to count on their fingers. We use our minds. Not some foreign swindle device. I am horrified. Absolutely horrified." I could see she was horrified. Her mouth pinched and she held the abacus away from her like it stunk. "You take your slate and coat and go home. And do not come back. I will not teach a cheater." She let the abacus fall. It split apart when it hit the dirt floor. The bright little beads flew in all directions.

Poor Zi. He looked at me and I shook my head. He'd never cheat, I was sure. Still, there was no way to prove it. He picked up his slate and reached under the desk top. His notebook was the only thing in there he'd want but Miss Steele stopped him before he could take it. "Go on," she said. "Get your coat."

He did and went sadly to the door. "Tomorrow?" he asked.

"No, not tomorrow. Not the next day or any day. I wash my hands of you."

"Don't go, Zi," Nora called. And then, as he did, "Come back soon."

Miss Steele stepped over and gave her a shake. "What I need for you, Missy, is a parrot cage. I would put you inside it and throw a cloth over it and you would be silenced." Of course the kids laughed. Nora ran and put her head in Bridgey's lap and wept.

My desk and bench were too small when Zi shared them. We kept bumping elbows. Or heads. With him gone it felt huge, too big and cold for one boy alone. He'd never get back in the school unless I found a way to let the teacher know what I knew. That Zi was as far beyond the rest of us as his talking white bird was beyond the camp ravens.

Miss Steele started dictating words and definitions to copy down and memorize. The little kids were supposed to sit and listen while the rest of us wrote.

Nora, stirred up by Miss Steele's threat about the parrot cage, couldn't sit quiet. First she got scolded because she whispered. Then she got scolded for jiggling around. Then she jostled little Annie Volk right off the bench. When Annie hit the floor she wet her drawers and went to howling.

Miss Steele said, "Nora, you are impossible today. I have had more than enough of your nonsense. Bring me your coat!" Nora crouched down on the floor whispering to Annie, likely saying she was sorry. She was always sorry after she caused trouble.

"You can't send her home alone in this weather, 'tis too bad out," Bridgey said. Hail tapped on the tin roof. Thunder like sometimes shakes the mountains during a spring snowstorm rolled overhead. Even that didn't soften Miss Steele's hard heart.

"Nora, bring me your coat," she said again. "This instant." That time Nora heard and did as she was told. The room got dead still as we waited for the teacher to slash Nora's little hands with her ruler. Instead she said, "Put your coat on and button it up."

"You can't send her home without her mittens and shawl." Bridgey's words simmered with anger.

She might as well have stayed silent. Miss Steele wasn't going to admit she'd heard her. She led Nora to the coat wall and picked her up and hung her on one of the pegs by the back of her coat collar. Nora gave her one unbelieving look and broke out in tears, her feet and fists drumming the wall. "I'm not a coat. I'm not a shawl. Put me down on the floor!"

"Be still, you scamp, or I will rap your legs with my ruler."

Nora stopped kicking and pounding. She sobbed once and then hung silent though tears kept rolling down her red cheeks. Annie crouched by the stove with her dress held up, drying off.

Miss Steele strode to her desk, her cheeks as red as Nora's and stood glaring, so angry even Bridgey didn't dare question what she'd done. There wasn't a word from anybody, only the wood snapping in the stove and sleet slapping the roof. Now and then Annie or Nora sniffed.

The teacher took up her book and went on with her dictation. Every sentence she read out cracked like a whip.

I put up with Nora's silent tears as long as I could. Then I went and lifted her off the coat peg. Miss Steele stopped reading. "What are you doing?"

"She's been punished enough."

"That is not for you to decide. Put her back where she was." I set Nora on the floor and reached for my coat. She clung to me while I put it on. I picked her up and held her in front of me as I carried her out, hunched with dread lest the ruler cut across my back.

I carried her till she got too heavy, then set her down. Behind us our schoolmates poured onto the schoolyard. Miss Steele had called recess like she always did when things got out of hand.

We walked silently through the sleet toward camp, trouble behind us and trouble ahead. Leaving school without the teacher's say-so was about as bad as a kid could get.

As we passed along Main Street below Mrs. Maynard's house, Zi hollered for us to come up. To put off facing Mam, we went. He showed us into the outdoor kitchen. His da gave one look at Nora and handed her a wet cloth to wipe her blotchy face.

I told Zi I thought Miss Steele had been watching for a reason to throw him out. He nodded, seeming to only half listen. "Will you please come with me? There is something I must show you."

Nora started to follow but Mr. Wong handed her a slice of pie and she settled back to enjoy it on a chair by the warm stove. For weeks I'd been telling at home the good things Mr. Wong gave me to eat. At last she had a chance to find out if I'd told true. She opened her mouth to take the first bite but instead asked," Is it Thursday?"

"It is," Zi said.

"Then we got to go, Ren, so I can deliver Miss Hettie's beautiful pies."

"She doesn't want you till after school. That's a long time yet. I'll get you there on time." She grinned, and went to work on the mince pie.

Zi and I ran to the carriage house and up the outside stairs. "Wait there in the doorway a minute," he said scratching a match, holding it to a lamp. The black, windowless room came to life with the light. On every wall hung scrolls with designs and painted pictures. And cloths embroidered like the one they'd given Mam. My eyes could hardly take in all that color, used as they were to the brown log walls of our cabin. "What are these for?" I asked.

"They will pay for my education, or to live on if Mrs. Maynard can no longer help us." He stood by the lamp holding one hand shut. "Look at this," he said. When he opened his fist my heart squeezed tight with fear. A fancy pin glittered on his palm. 'Twas plain 'twas the one that belonged to Mrs. Paunce. Sis had stretched the truth. There weren't seventeen diamonds, only twelve, but they were big and sparkly. The emerald shone bright as the lamp.

I asked, "How come you have it?" knowing as I spoke it might be a useless question. How did I know if telling the truth was a thing Chinese stuck by?

"I cleaned Star's cage when I came home. This lay in her nest. It must have been there ever since she came back after Finn drove her away."

"You mean she put it there? Not somebody else, to get you in trouble?"

"I cannot be certain but I suspect she was the thief. Once she flew into a store and flew out with a silver chain. If Mrs. Paunce was mistaken about locking up and if a window stood open, Star would have been attracted." It sounded like the truth. "I shrink at telling the Paunces what happened and saying how sorry I am."

"You can't do that. 'Twould be awful."

"Why? Is that not what an American boy should do?"

"Wait" I said. "Just listen. You're mixed up about this American boy stuff. I'm no more American than you. I'm Irish. My mam and da are Irish. Someday maybe we'll be Americans but we aren't yet. I don't even know how you get to be one."

Zi just shrugged. "You did not explain why I should not go to the Paunces."

"There's a push on in camp against sinfulness and crime. Parents are tired of guarding their kids from bad examples and what they own from getting stole. They'd love to catch a thief and tar and feather him for a warning. Should you take back the pin, they'll think you took it. No matter how hard you explain, they'll likely not believe what you say. But should they hear you out and you escape the noose, they'll kill Star. They're that angry." We stood staring down at the hateful brooch till I thought to ask, "Does your father know about it?"

He shook his head. "I do not wish him to know. He would hurry over and hand it to the Paunces and accept the blame for stealing it to protect Star and me. That is why I waited to ask you the best way to get it where it belongs. I cannot keep something that is not mine." And Miss Steele had the crust to say he'd cheat! "Should I put it into a box and mail it back?" he asked.

"That'd mean going into the post office. The postmaster might suspicion something when he saw the address. People in Miner's Chance don't mail each other things, it costs too much. They just pass things over."

"Should I tell Mrs. Maynard? She would under-stand." I could just imagine Mrs. Maynard, sure and unruffled, walking next door and handing the brooch back to the Paunces. I could also imagine Mr. Paunce asking where she got it. She'd gall enough to say, "Never you mind," and walk on home. But the Paunces'd never let her get away with that, the mine owners being rivals. What if they called the marshal, the closest thing we had to a lawman, and he made her swear on a Bible how she came by the pin?

"Don't tell anybody. Just shut up a minute. Let me work it over." I was trying to do as Mam bade me, use my head. And sure enough, a answer came. "I know. There's one person can return the pin and not say where he got it."

"Who?"

"Father Fergus. The priest at our church. Nobody could make him tell who he got it from."

"Why not?" I told him how us Catholics confessed the things we'd done wrong to the priest every Satur-day. And how our priests vowed never to blab anything told them.

"Not even to the marshal or in a court?"

"Not to the marshal and Miner's Chance hasn't got a court. Give me the pin. As soon as I can I'll find Father Fergus and tell him what's happened." This wasn't only about a stolen brooch. 'Twas about people looking for somebody to blame. A lot of them would be happy to blame Zi and his da whether or not they'd done wrong.

"I am very fortunate and grateful to have you to explain American ways to me!" He helped me pin the brooch inside my jacket.

Nora was in a swivet when I gathered her up from the outdoor kitchen. She knew she was late and told me so all the way to Miss Hettie's. But when we opened the door there, the smell of spices and baking fruit flooded out. The pies still bubbled in her oven.

"Is Nora doing her job all right?" I asked. "Is she old enough for what you want of her?" 'Twas a lot for a six-year-old, being trusted with delivering pies.

Miss Hettie smiled and her big, square teeth seemed to burst open her wrinkled face. "Any older and she'd be careless. Any younger and she'd not have the strength."

"What if some boy snatches one?"

Miss Hettie thumped a plate of cookies on the table in front of us. "Nobody in Miner's Chance is going to let a little girl get robbed of a pie. There'd be a hue and a cry like to raise the dead and one sad boy taught a painful lesson."

The brooch weighed heavier and heavier as I walked away. I found myself peering behind me lest somebody come creeping up and discover what I carried. When I got home I pinned it to my pallet and drew my bed-clothes over it.

Before I left again for the livery stable, I told Mam I'd defied Miss Steele and why. She spent all her fury bad-mouthing the teacher and saved none for me. "It's that soft heart of yours heading you into trouble again, poor lad," she ended up. "This time 'twas a blessing. Though, we'll all be happier does the tale not come to the ears of your da."

"Wouldn't he want Nora rescued from being hung up like a rabbit at the butcher's shack?"

"Of course he would."

"Didn't I stand up to Miss Steele? He keeps saying I ought to stand up to people."

"Yes, but 'tis why you did it that will ruffle him," Mam said. "You took Nora down because you felt sorry for her, not to defy Miss Steele. Didn't you?"

"Yes, but . . ."

"He doesn't want you swayed by feelings. He thinks they muddle your good sense."

"Even so he doesn't have to hate me."

"You're blind, lad. He doesn't hate you. He's after you lately because he fears for you. When he was your age, back in the old country, his da drove him out to make his own way in the world because there wasn't food enough for all. He never saw his young brothers and sisters again. He'd not know them should he pass them on the street. So he looks at you and asks hisself, 'Has Renny the grit to make his own way as I did at his age? Were I killed in the mine, is he strong enough to provide for his mam and sisters?' And his answer to hisself is, 'No, he's too soft to fight his way. He needs toughening.' "

"I'm tired of his toughening. I'm tired of Mr.

McMinn punching me. I'm tired that Da never smiles his special smile at me like he used to."

"Then look at his hands, scarred by digging a living for us out of the earth, and forgive him," Mam said. "Worry that we might starve snaps at his heels every day of his life. But let's talk of it no more. And don't repeat his story to the girls, 'tis too ugly."

I wished she hadn't told me. I felt sorry for the boy Da had been and could understand why he wanted a brawling, tough son. But I wasn't like that.

Knowing what he wanted from me, I was sure I'd fail him.

8

A Favorite Goes to Jail

I found Father Fergus watching some men notch logs where our gulch opened into Main Street. That's where he'd decided to put the new church. The workmen weren't close enough to hear what I said to him. So I asked right there, "Should somebody confess something awful to you, could the marshal make you tell who did it?"

"No. But surely, Renny, you haven't done anything Marshal Jenks would be interested in, have you?"

"Not me, Father. A friend of mine."

"Then why are you here? Why isn't he asking?"

"'Tis mixed up but I think you'll see why if I tell it all." So I told it all.

By the time I finished he was nodding his head. "You are right to be concerned for the boy. If this became known the Wongs would be in real trouble, even in danger."

"If I bring you the pin, could you get it back with no trouble to yourself?"

"Of course," he said. "Bring it to my boardinghouse. Worry no more about it."

I took it to him and didn't worry anymore. But I should have. Because when he took the Paunces the brooch, they tried to make him tell who he'd got it from. They knew he hadn't stole it, but they wanted to know who did.

"You know I can't break the seal of the confessional," is what Father Fergus was reported afterwards to have said.

And Mr. Paunce was reported to have answered right back, "We can't let a second-story burglar walk loose."

Father Fergus went back to Mrs. Felter's boarding-house, Mr. Paunce calling after him, "Don't blame me if I have to make an example of you." Likely he'd not have been so hard had Father Fergus and the bishop let him build a stone church named for Mrs. Paunce and Sis.

Zi being gone, the Paunce kids came back to school. That added to my gloom. Cedric kept saying how good it was he didn't have to worry anymore about catching the Chinese rot. And Sis kept telling everybody, "So stupid, him thinking he can be an American boy. He hasn't even got an American face."

Each afternoon Zi waited at Mrs. Maynard's gate for me to tell him what I remembered of the day's school-work. Some days I was able to copy down problems for him on pages I tore from his little notebook. I felt like a spy stealing secrets right under the nose of the enemy.

If there was no schoolwork he could do, we'd sit in the upstairs room and he'd tell me stories about the scrolls and embroidered pictures. Or about the village he'd come from, what they worked at, their animals and pets, how they celebrated things. His words made it so clear I heard cymbals crash and watched fireworks shake different colored stars out of the black sky.

When he asked me to tell about Ireland, suddenly I smelled peat smoke in mist, and heard the shish, shish of waves against the shore. I couldn't put that into words. So I told him about Boston where we'd stayed when we first came and I'd been picked on for being Irish by some boys bigger than me. I'd been four then, them maybe five and six.

One afternoon I headed down Main Street to buy Mam some salt. I was passing Mrs. Felter's boarding-house when out she dashed onto her porch. She screamed, "Help! Help!" as sharp and startling as the whistle at the Kitkat. Bridgey's scared face pressed against a upstairs window.

The screams drew a crowd. Riders pulled their horses to a halt. A freighter slowed, the driver standing up to drag on the reins. I looked for smoke curling out the windows, fire being the thing everybody feared most, but didn't see any. Mrs. Felter went on screaming. She pointed toward the door.

The marshal came out of the boardinghouse leading Father Fergus. The little priest bowed right and left in his kindly way like he was setting out on a afternoon stroll. But nobody goes for a stroll with the marshal watching every step to see they don't bolt. "Be silent, Mrs. Felter," the marshal said. Her screams dwindled down to sobs.

"What's he done wrong?" somebody asked.

"Bless him, he's never done a wrong deed in his life." Mrs. Brodie stepped from the crowd and stamped up the boardinghouse steps, her empty egg basket swinging on her arm. She was near tall as the marshal. The stair rails quivered with her passing. She grabbed hold of the lawman's lapel. "What are you doing to the good Father?"

Marshal Jenks was the picture of what a lawman ought to look like, wide in the shoulders and sure of hisself. But my da said he hadn't any brain bigger than a chipmunk's. I guess Da knew. A smarter man would have taken the priest in the late night when law abiding folk weren't around to ask questions. And he wouldn't have clamped those manacles on the priest's wrists, either.

Mrs. Brodie jerked the marshal's lapel again and a button pinged on the porch. "What's this you're doing, then?" We drew closer to hear his answer. Every eye glared at the marshal like he was the criminal.

It maybe seemed to Marshal Jenks that the crowd meant to move against him. He pulled back from Mrs. Brodie and slapped his hand to his holster. "Now see here. You've no cause to come menacing me when I'm doing my duty. Mr. Paunce signed a complaint against the priest and it's up to me to jail him till the thing's settled."

Many in the camp thought the priest a saint. Shouts resounded. "You can't hold him without a trial, just on somebody's say-so. Jail a priest? That's wicked! What is Paunce thinking of?" Their roar rattled the windows.

The driver of the freighter snapped his bullwhip with such a crack it silenced the crowd. "What's the charge against the priest?" he asked.

"Withholding evidence against a criminal. Mr. Paunce said he's to be held in jail until he tells who stole Mrs. Paunce's brooch."

Mrs. Brodie turned to the crowd. "Of course he'd withhold it. Hasn't every priest swore to keep secrets to hisself?"

Father Fergus stepped in front of the marshal. "Don't berate Marshal Jenks," he said, patting Mrs. Brodie's arm. "'Twas a waste to hire ourselves a lawman unless we let him do his job. Go on home, now. This is less important than you're making out. It will be solved in no time."

But the crowd was in a angry mood, calling threats. A mud ball splattered against the steps. Father Fergus talked earnestly to Mr. Jenks. At last the marshal unlocked the manacles from the priest's wrists. The priest held up his hands for silence. When the crowd kept shouting, he shouted louder. He had a huge voice for such a splinter of a man. "You know some of us are working hard, trying to bring law and order to Miner's Chance. With people of all stripes, good and bad, crowding into camp, each of us needs to help fight crime.

Move aside and let us pass so the marshal can do his part in that and I can do mine."

"We don't want you locked up," a man from the assay office called.

"Then you're not on the side of my bishop," Father Fergus said. "He keeps writing that I'm too busy and need more time in solitude. Jail will take care of that."

His little joke punched a hole in people's anger and they quieted down. They pulled back to let the marshal lead the priest past. "We'll see you don't stay there," they called, shaking their heads at the injustice of it. He'd taken his own food to many when they were hungry, or carried his stove wood to them when they were cold. Had there been a vote in camp on who was most loved, he'd likely have won it.

"Don't you worry, Father," Mrs. Brodie called. "We'll get the teacher lady to write this all down on paper and send it to the bishop. He'll see you're done right by."

"Bless you," Father Fergus said, "but you mustn't do that. Our poor bishop, saddled with a diocese as big as all outdoors, having to stop the important things he has to do and come settle this? Don't do it. I beg you."

"Well, if you say so," Mrs. Brodie said. You could tell she wasn't happy about it but she'd never go against the priest.

In all that crowd I bet no one felt so bad about him getting locked up as I did. I'd caused it, asking him to return the brooch. My heart heavy as a ore bucket, I walked to the lean-to built on the side of the marshal's house. I called and Father Fergus came to the barred window. "'Tis awful, you jailed because of me, Father."

He smiled. "I know you feel that way, lad. But don't look so sad. Being here will give me extra time for prayers. Miner's Chance needs a lot of them right now."

"I can get you free if I tell how the pin really got stole." I'd be a traitor to Zi if I did that, but a traitor to Father Fergus if I didn't.

"No, no. Stand by the Wongs. Promise you will." I promised, his serious face showing he thought it important. "Anyway, my getting jailed may be a good thing."

"How could it be?"

"You know how people have talked nothing but law and order for months?" I nodded. "Have you wondered why they just talk and don't go ahead and elect a mayor and write some laws?" I shook my head. "Because some would have to give up things they're free to do now. Mr. Paunce couldn't slap people he disagrees with in jail without a trial. Your da couldn't decide everything with a fistfight."

"Maybe did you tell them . . ."

He smiled. "They have to want the law because they see they need it, not because I tell them they need it. Remember two years back when this was a raw, brawling settlement? That man fool enough to brag of the nuggets he'd found, murdered for them? Men strung up for claim jumping? We're not that wild anymore but we're not a safe, peaceful place, either. My jailing may be the thing that points that out." Then he began preaching to me about how Miner's Chance could grow into a real town, fair to all. How it could have a two-story brick school and a library and maybe even a train coming in, and no more holdups night or day.

I had to stand stiff not to twitch or let my eyes glaze over, he went on so long. Finally he ended up, "Meantime, the weaker will be ground down by those stronger, unless someone sticks up for them as you've stuck up for your friend, Zi. So keep doing it. Now run along and don't come back. Somebody seeing you here might guess it's you I'm shielding."

I kicked a stone ahead of me as I walked from the jail. Father Fergus was right. In our camp the strongest won whether 'twas lawful and orderly or not.

The arrest of Father Fergus set Miner's Chance to boiling. Main Street filled with knots of people talking angry. Some miners from the Kitkat threatened to strike. Others warned them not to. "Paunce'll just wire Denver for strikebreakers," they said, "then where'll we be?"

Finn told everybody at school to shun Sis and Cedric or else they'd have him to deal with. The Brodies got half their food from Father Fergus.

'Twas during that troubled time that Mrs. Maynard and Miss Steele had their big abacus battle. Mrs. Maynard started it, arriving at school carrying a box. We were eating our lunch inside, sunshine having warmed the schoolyard to inch-deep mud. So we listened in on everything the ladies said to each other.

Our teacher's face set when she saw who came in but she stood up and offered Mrs. Maynard a chair. Mrs. Maynard sat down with her box on her knee. "I have come to ask you to try an experiment," she said. Miss Steele's cold look mustn't have given her much hope but she went on, "There is an abacus here for each child in the school. I had Mr. Wong make them. I will be glad to teach the children to use them. You will see their understanding of arithmetic increase dramatically, I am sure."

"You ask me to teach my students to cheat?" Miss Steele's voice sounded as shocked as though Mrs. Maynard asked her to teach us to pick pockets.

"Is giving them help with their studies teaching them to cheat?"

"I believe so if it is that particular kind of help."

Mrs. Maynard took a deep breath and began again. "As a whole, are the boys or the girls best at arithmetic?"

"The boys this year. Except some."

"May I, then, train the girls in the use of an abacus, and see in two weeks, if they catch up to the boys?"

"You are trying to get that Chinaman of yours back in my school," Miss Steele said.

"And you are trying to keep him out." They'd forgotten us. They were shooting each other with words. "Of course, Zi could help anyone having difficulty with this valuable teaching tool," Mrs. Maynard said.

"Teaching tool. Ha! Cheating tool."

"I think you believe that, Miss Steele. I have no doubt of your integrity. But is a slate or a book or a map any less of a cheating tool? There is so much for the children to learn. They need every help. To assist a child to learn is the greatest gift anyone can give." Even though I didn't much like Miss Steele, I knew Mrs. Maynard didn't have to tell her that. 'Twas clear to all she really did want to teach us.

"You are trying to sweet-talk me, Mrs. Maynard. I will not be bamboozled."

Mrs. Maynard laughed. "Bamboozled, that funny old-fashioned word." She laughed again. We all laughed.

"Bamboozled, bamboozled." The little ones rolled the new word around on their tongues.

Miss Steele dropped down on her chair. "Do you really think it would help them understand better?" She looked at Finn and at Hedda Volk, her eyes worried. But then she blinked like waking from a dream. Her face set again. "Nobody tells me how to run my classroom, Mrs. Maynard. Thank you for bringing the abacuses. We shall not be using them."

"I have vowed to myself that I shall get Zi educated," Mrs. Maynard told her. "I will do so if I have to close the Rejoice and move somewhere else." The kids whose fathers worked at her gold mine suddenly sat very still.

"I have vowed to provide these children with the best education of which I am capable," Miss Steele said. "The boy gave nothing but trouble. School was in an uproar when he was here. No, he may not come back."

Mrs. Maynard bit her lip and took up her box and left.

About that time Mam began nagging at me. "Stand up straight, lad. I've never known you to slump so." But I'd forget and she'd say it again. If only I could have told her what worried me. Would I go to Hell for getting a priest sent to jail? There was nobody I dared ask. Father Fergus had said to stay away from the jail and 'twas no use questioning the only one I could talk to, Zi.

He'd not know, not being Catholic.

9

All My Fault

The men weren't singing that Friday night when I went to the Green Eyes after Da. They stood talking so low and serious 'twas scary, the saloon usually being such a noisy, cheerful place. They stared at me there between the doors. I expected Mr. Brodie to say, "'Tis not near time for you to go, Lon," like he said every Friday. He didn't.

Da spoke, his face too stern for me to ask him any questions. "You go on home. I'll be late coming." I backed out and went across to lean against the newspaper office, wondering what was up.

The night dentist shoved one of his barrels over for me to sit on. He asked, "Have they decided over there what they're going to do?"

"I didn't hear what they're talking over."

"To strike or not."

"I thought they'd decided not to," I said, irked that this stranger knew something about the Irish miners I didn't. "How come you know about it?"

"Sitting here every night I see and hear all that goes

on, like this affair of the mine owner making their priest a prisoner. They can't let him get away with that."

"But strike and maybe lose their jobs?" The dentist just shrugged. Father Fergus was right. The camp needed prayers.

The doors of the Green Eyes slammed open and out shoved the miners. They stormed up the middle of the street like 'twas empty. Horse traffic pulled to the side of the wide roadway making room. On the boardwalks, people stopped to watch the miners pass.

"Looks like they've decided, boy," the night dentist said. "You'd best go on home. There're bad times ahead."

I knew he spoke true and I remember how guilty his words made me feel. If I hadn't got Father Fergus sent to jail this wouldn't have happened.

I tagged after the miners. By the time they came below the Paunces' cold-looking stone house, their number had grown to twice its size. They surged up the path and milled around the metal fountain in the Paunces' front yard like they were making up their minds. Then Da went up the steps and clanged the door knocker. The sound of it rang inside my head, knock, knock, your fault, your fault.

The door of the mansion swung open and there stood Sis, light from inside outlining her ruffles and curls and bows. Main Street had grown so quiet, Da's words to her came clear through the cold night air. "We're here to speak to Mr. Paunce, Miss."

"He's at supper." A servant loomed behind her and they talked. They must have seen things were serious. She left and the servant stood holding the door half open.

In a minute she came back and said, "Papa says he'll come when he's finished his coffee."

"Say he's to come now or we'll come in," Da said. Sis ran back down the hall calling.

In a trice the door banged back and Mr. Paunce stood there. "I detest being pestered at meals. What is it?"

Da took off his cap. "We want the priest freed. He's done no wrong."

"He's holding back evidence against a criminal. It's time all in camp start keeping the law, even him."

"Being a priest, he can't do else but guard his secret. But if lawfulness is what you're after, what of yourself? 'Tis not lawful holding a man with no trial." Mr. Paunce picked his teeth with his little finger like what was caught there mattered more than Da's accusing words. "If 'tis a scapegoat you want, lock me up in his place, and let him out," Da said. "The camp needs him."

"That's just like one of you lazy Irish, looking for a chance to loll in jail and escape working."

"Ah, you're a snake," Da said, "trying to forget, since you struck gold, that you're Irish as the rest of us under that fine white shirt of yours. Don't turn against your own people. Give us back our priest."

"The answer is no. Now get your rabble off my property," Mr. Paunce said.

Da raised his fist. The miners must have been watching for that. They raised their fists, too, and shouted, "Strike! Strike! Strike!" The sound bounced back from the other side of the canyon, Strike! Strike! Strike!

Mr. Paunce raised his own fist and thundered, "To Hell with that. I'll get strikebreakers in here that will do twice the work you do." A growl rose from the crowd.

"Don't think you're going to telegraph for them," Da said. "The wireless office is guarded and guarded 'twill be night and day. Likewise the post office. Ride off in your fancy carriage to Denver and lead scabs back if you want. But sure that shelf road is a easy one to blockade. It'll be weeks before you fight your way to your mine. You'll do better to let Father Fergus go. We'll take up our tools as soon as he's set free."

Mr. Paunce's voice rose so high it cracked, "Do what you like. We'll see who wins." He signaled his servant to slam the door. Oh, Da, I thought, in the camps the owners always win.

There followed a time that hurt everybody. The striking miners hadn't the money to buy at the slab shacks on Main Street, making the storekeepers suffer. As did the theater, saloons, tobacco shop, every place with something to sell. Traffic on Main Street fell way off. Zig-zagging across it was easy.

The boardwalks were the opposite, hard to push through, so many idle miners and drivers lounged along them. For sure, the Rejoice went full swing, its whistle reminding each morning that some people still had to work. But Miner's Chance was like a man with one leg gone, everything was off balance.

After the strike had been going a week, business got so slow at the livery stable and the boardinghouse that Bridgey and me were let go. I took the news of my firing with a grin. No more fisticuffs! Hearing from Zi that I was out of work, Mrs. Maynard asked me to care for her horses, the prettiest bays in camp. After feeding and watering the whole livery stable, doing just two was easy.

In a few days Mr. McMinn sent word I might as well come on back for my sparring lessons. So few people were renting hacks he needed something to do. Every afternoon I'd have to drag down there. We'd wrap the cloths around our hands and go at it, him the boxer and me the punching bag. Then, one day I was thinking how wrong everything was and I socked him back so hard his cigar flew out of his mouth onto the floor. It set some straw to smoldering. "I'm sorry, I'm sorry," I cried stamping it out.

"No. You finally stood up for yourself. I feared you'd go on letting me drub you forever. Good lad! Your da will be proud," he was working his jaw back and forth to see if it still hung together.

"Is that what Da means when he talks of standing up to people—doing right by yourself?" I'd thought there was more bluff and bluster in it, showing everybody you were better than them.

"He meant to respect yourself. Not let bullies treat you like a worm. Now let's go at it again. Having found your gumption, I'll be able to teach you some street-fighting tricks."

Meantime, little Nora was the only one of us kids that kept bringing home money. She'd go through camp delivering for Miss Hettie, careful as though the pie was diamonds. Even jobless men bought pies because they tasted like home. Or because it gave them a chance to talk to a little kid who reminded them of ones they'd left behind.

Da acted like a angry bull around the house those days. He couldn't sit quiet or still his tongue, arguing with Mam as if she took Mr. Paunce's side. "You might use your free time digging me a well," she said, finally. He did start but couldn't keep at it. He needed to pace around and throw up his arms and talk with other strikers. Down to the Green Eyes he'd go, Mam calling after him, "You make one tot of whiskey last all afternoon. And don't you go treating the others. The families have need of food, not drink."

Miners always tread the edge of starvation. We weren't as bad off as most, since Mam's lace was so prized, ladies waited in line to buy it. Others from our gulch weren't that lucky. When Mrs. Brodie sent Kevin down to borrow a cup of meal, Mam gave him a bowlful. "Should you meet my man and he asks you where that come from, don't you say 'tis from here," Mam cautioned him.

"Da'll mislike you giving our food away," Bridgey warned.

"He'd better not find it out from you, Miss," Mam answered and told her to ask Doreen and Finn to stop for a bite on the way from school.

"Not Finn," Bridgey said.

"Especially Finn," Mam said. "You need to practice loving your fellow man."

"Before I'd love that Finn . . . ," Bridgey started but Mam silenced her with a look.

One morning Jules couldn't answer a question Miss Steele asked him. She said, "Think, boy, think!"

"I'm too hungry to think." He put his head down on his desk and his shoulders lurched.

I'd not have believed it of Old Steele but the next morning she said, "Learning shall go on here whether there is a strike or not. I have set a bushel of apples next to the drinking pail. If you are hungry go eat so we can get on with our work."

Kids rushed for those apples. Not the Paunces, of course, or the ones whose fathers worked at the Rejoice. Nora started up but Bridgey grabbed her and made her go back to her bench. I sat and read Zi's notebook:

> Sis is a sad person. Each day she makes
> another attempt to edge her way in but no
> one will have her. She puts the children
> off by trying to show them how much better
> she is than they are. Her jewelry and
> fancy clothes and fine toys are her burdens
> of proof. For her, school has become a
> little world of closed faces and deaf ears.

That made me really look at Sis. Maybe she was lonely. Was that why she picked at everybody?

Miss Steele hadn't thought what a stomach full of apples would do to those hungry kids' insides. The whole afternoon hands waved asking leave to rush to the outhouse. Next day she brought a small barrel of crackers.

I kept reading bits of Zi's notebook when Miss Steele hadn't her eyes on me. I'd said I'd bring it home to him but he said, "No. Write in it sometimes. It will make a record for me of the school year." So I added notes here and there. Not that they came near the word pictures he made of people like:

> How Finn dreads reading! He seems to
> shrink. Sis's scornful snorts are
> daggers in his back. The teacher asks
> him to try harder. His neck flushes red.
> Every muscle stretches tight. But
> nothing comes out of his mouth. He is
> blind to reading.

He wrote a lot, too, about the things his da told him.

> Father warns me not to let the teasing
> change me. They are acting like boys
> everywhere, picking on the one they
> consider weakest. He says Finn
> deserves my pity because society
> has shoved him to the bottom and may
> always hold him there and he is afraid.

Zi had written something about everybody in school. He'd described Nora's funny ways, and Bridgey and Doreen both pretty but so different, and how Annie Volk was like a new kitten taken too soon from its mother.

As she did now and then, one afternoon the teacher made us clean our desks. We set everything on top and dusted underneath with a rag she handed us. She cast a mistrustful eye on what we laid out, like we might be hiding dynamite sticks under our desk tops.

When she came to me I swiped around while she looked over the things I'd set out. There wasn't much. Just penwipers and pens, a stone with a extra lot of mica layered in it, and a shed snakeskin. I'd left Zi's little notebook hid where she wouldn't see it. But then I thought, things can't get worse between them. If anything will change her mind about him, it'll be that notebook. So I laid it out. She made me put the snakeskin in the stove and reached to pick the notebook up. "What is this?"

"It belongs to Zi."

"Another thing to help him cheat?"

"Mrs. Maynard gave it to him so he'd not waste school time. He practiced his English in it."

She looked like she doubted what I said. As she leafed through the pages the kids fixed their eyes on me, wondering what I'd done now. "I shall read through this. There better not be anything smutty in it." She went back to her desk and announced, "Recess time. Outside all of you. Quickly!" just like she'd planned all along for us to take time out right them. We put on our wraps and went into the muddy schoolyard, grumbling.

The burro train came ambling past on its way down from the Rejoice. Mornings somebody herded them. Afternoons they were let loose to graze on their way back to Main Street. "Quick," Finn said. "Hold open the gate."

We ran out on the road and formed a line across it. Finn and Kevin ran at the burros, waving their arms, heading them into the schoolyard. The pretty little animals were used to kids, not wild. The gate clicked shutting them in and we climbed on. Every big kid got one except Sis, who said we'd all stink of burro.

She stood under the tree with the little ones, brushing them away from her like they were flies. They were used to that from Sis but whined about not getting to ride till Doreen said, "Watch the door. You'll be first to know, does Teacher drop in a blue faint when she sees us."

We paraded waving branches to make it fancy, the little ones clapping. Finn's burro kept trying to break out of line and that started races. We circled the school two at a time, mud flying up on the one behind. Every minute we expected to hear a shriek from Miss Steele and the bell clanging to get us back in.

Jules finally beat us all and showed his burro out the gate. Others sent their mounts down the road and started scraping off the mud, laughing. Sis scolded

Cedric. "Look at you, muddy as a miner's brat. What will you tell Mama?"

"That I never had more fun. That I'm tired of always having to act proper, nowadays. That I wish Papa hadn't struck gold and I didn't have to watch how I talk."

"You better not. You'll get horsewhipped," Sis said.

Bridgey said, "Let's go back in. Teacher never made us stay out so long. Maybe she's been taken with a faint inside, from hearing us race about."

We clattered in. Miss Steele sat with Zi's notebook open. She looked up with surprise like she'd forgot there were kids in the Miner's Chance school. Her eyes were red and so was her long nose. I'd have thought she'd been crying didn't I know what a hard heart she had.

The rest of the afternoon went like always except at the end Miss Steele called me to her desk. I went expecting a tongue-lashing but she asked, "Where does Mrs. Maynard work during the day?"

"In a office behind her house."

"I would like you to take me there." I felt like a prisoner walking with her down the road. The kids hung back. There wasn't a whisper from them. I could almost feel their puzzlement about where Miss Steele was marching me to.

Zi told me later the teacher and Mrs. Maynard talked for a long time. They called him in and asked him to write some things. I guess Miss Steele wanted to make sure Zi wrote the things in the notebook. When it seemed certain he did, she went off to think out what it meant.

Two days later Zi came back to school. Miss Steele had decided he ought to get a education. After that when he put up his hand he got called on. She poured facts down him like he was a empty well.

Mr. Paunce and other parents complained about him coming back, but he stayed. No one was going to tell Miss Steele how to run her school.

Meantime, Father Fergus still paced back and forth in the jail. In spite of the prayers he must have been praying, things in Miner's Chance just got worse.

10

The Attack on the School

One night the mountain lion that lived on Ute Peak came through camp and carried off Dr. Applegate's tortoiseshell cat. When the doctor saw milk still in the cat's dish next morning and blood on the ground, he knew what happened. He put a notice in the newspaper that pets should be inside before night and not let loose in the morning. He forgot to say about the lion. There were whispers the Chinese took the cat to eat. Two stores put signs in their windows: NO CHINAMEN SERVED HERE.

We talked about it when Bridgey brought the news home. "New people in camp don't know about lions," Mam said. "Saying Chinese ate the cat makes more sense to them than what's true."

"It wouldn't did they know Zi and his da," I said.

Nora said, "They'd not do that. I know."

Bridgey asked, "How do you know? Didn't Mr. Wong give you mincemeat pie? He could have made that out of cat."

Nora turned gray around her mouth. "I think maybe I'm going to throw up."

"I think maybe you're not," Mam said.

And I said to Bridgey, "That was regular mincemeat, dummy. I ate some too."

"You can make mincemeat with any kind of meat."

"You hush, Bridget. Of course it wasn't cat," Mam said. "The lion took the doctor's tortoiseshell cat just like lions took other pets before." Bridgey made the kind of face that said, I know I'm right.

Another thing happened that got people talking against Zi and his da. It started one Saturday. Warm spring days had caused purple pasqueflowers to uncurl from under the last of the snow. Nora went gathering them. Suddenly she burst into the cabin and stood against the door panting, her eyes scared, like she'd just escaped being caught by somebody. "What is it?" Mam asked.

"Something by the new church." Mam went on raising and turning her bobbins. She hadn't seen Nora's eyes.

"You want to show me?" I asked. Nora took my hand and we tramped down through the woods. When we neared the end of the path she pointed and I saw it. Overnight a bright tent had been raised up there. Little flags fluttered along its top edges.

"See?" Nora asked, her arms wrapped tight around her. "Maybe 'tis gypsies. Mayo and Mab said gypsies steal kids."

"That's fool talk. Gypsies don't steal kids," I said. She gave me a sideways look checking that I really meant it. "Whoever they are they shouldn't be there by the church. You wait here. I'll find out about it." I walked on by myself.

The tent was huge. A pipe running through the top let out smoke that blew away in a gray trail. A buzz of voices hummed inside. Miners waited out front. "What's going on?" I asked one of them.

"Gambling. The Chinese kind. They call it FanTan. And there's pretty Chinese ladies." He smiled, swinging a bag of gold dust. "Too bad for you. Kids can't get in."

"I just want to look."

He shook his head. "You better go along."

I went back to Nora. "'Tis a Chinese gambling tent. Run tell Mam. She won't want you down here. I'm going to talk to Zi about it." I watched her hurry home through the trees. Worries swarmed in my head. More Chinese had come like Da feared they would if Zi and his da got to stay. Why now, when Zi was back in school, the kids had just about quit teasing, and it looked like Miner's Chance had given up fighting the Wongs?

I found Zi in the outside kitchen where he'd set up a table to practice his Chinese writing. I told him about the tent. He began talking fast to his da. His da talked fast back.

"My father cannot say until he goes to look. He fears they may be men who were driven out of Denver. Signs telling about them were posted everywhere when we passed through there. They were ousted for cheating their patrons. And selling opium."

"The man I talked to said there were pretty ladies, too," I said.

"Good Chinese women don't work in gambling tents," Zi said. Mr. Wong kept breaking out in excited talk.

When Da warned that trouble would follow if Zi and his da stayed in camp he meant labor trouble, Chinese taking the Irish miners' jobs. Chinese troubles did follow, sure enough, though not the kind Da expected. Arguments and fights raged all the time around that gambling tent, so different from at Gambler Jim's where things were kept on a tight rein. A miner got shot in the arm. Another lost his job, going to work at the Rejoice foggy with opium.

Angry talk about that shiny tent could be heard wherever I stopped to listen. Mam told Da, "You must do something. It worries me, the children passing by there when they come and go."

"I'm studying on it," he said. "When I get a plan thought through and the men organized to carry it out, we'll do one grand sweep and get those Chinese and all the other crooks and riffraff that's cluttering up the camp."

School was almost over one afternoon when the Rejoice paymaster handed a note in at the door. As the teacher read it her face clouded like the note was full of bad news. She laid it down and sat a minute with her lips pursed. Then she took the school key from its hook on the side of her desk and locked the door. "Aren't you going to let us out to go home?" Sis asked.

"Not yet," Miss Steele said. "Mrs. Maynard has been kind enough to warn me that there is trouble in camp. She suggested we stay late today." Annie Volk began to whimper. "We shall play games, Annie. Let us push the desks back and bring the benches into a circle." The boys did that with a lot of crashing. It sobered me that Miss Steele didn't throw in recess to get control. Something must be really wrong.

First we sang rounds. Then we told riddles. Then we had a spelling bee, mostly funny words that made us laugh: dunderhead, and tweet, and even bamboozle. Cedric spelled us all down as usual. "Can't we go outside?" Finn asked for at least the tenth time.

Miss Steele lost her patience. "You go sit on the punishment stool, Finn. I am tired of your complaining." Finn went, dragging his heels.

Miss Steele brought her latest copy of *St. Nicholas* magazine and began to read it out even though it wasn't Friday. Finn broke in, "Somebody's coming. A crowd. All plastered wet by the rain." He'd pulled moss from between the logs and made a peephole.

"Sit up straight," Miss Steele said. "It is none of your affair."

"Maybe they're headed up to the mine," Cedric said.

"No, sir, they ain't. They're coming in at the gate."

Knowing Finn, I thought he'd made that up to scare us. But there came a rattle at the latch and then a loud pounding on the door.

"Just sit quiet," Miss Steele whispered. "No need to answer it."

But there was need. The knocking made that plain. And the loud shouts. "Open up or we'll break the door." A body rammed against it.

Still Miss Steele whispered, "Just keep quiet, they will not harm us." Annie went to weeping and some of the other little ones joined in. Bridgey took Nora on her lap.

"Send out the Chinese kid," a voice called through the keyhole. "We want to see how he looks strung up by his pigtail." Everybody turned to Zi. He bit the inside of his cheek and stared past us at the door. For a moment 'twas quiet inside and out except for the tap of spring rain on the tin roof.

Miss Steele asked, "What are they doing now, Finn?"

"Gathering up rocks between swigs at their bottle. They're some of the out-of-work miners. 'Twill be bad if they get inside."

Zi said, "I will go out. I can take care of myself."

"You said that before," I told him. "It wasn't true then nor is it true now. We've got to stick together. All of us." I looked around at the kids. Their eyes slid away. Except Nora's. Except Bridgey's. Except Finn's.

A stone crashed through one of the high-up oiled paper windows and others pattered against the logs and rang on the roof. A cheer rose outside and inside Sis began to scream. "Papa told you he shouldn't be here," she accused Miss Steele, her voice shrill. "It's stupid having to go to school with a Chinaman."

"No more stupid than having to go to school with somebody who dresses like every day is Sunday," Bridgey said.

"You wouldn't know, never dressing proper yourself," Sis spat out.

"Shut up, you girls," Cedric said. He waved to Jules and they shoved some desks together making a barrier to hide behind. The Paunces had as much to fear from the miners as Zi did.

He pushed past the desks. "I must go out as they ask. It will be best for everyone if I do."

"No, Zi," Nora cried. I tried to drag him back from the door but he kicked out and caught my knee and I doubled up with the pain of it.

"Stop it, all of you," Miss Steele said, slashing around with her metal ruler. She caught me and Cedric and Jules on our clothes but Zi turned and the ruler traced a scratch from his eye to his chin.

"Look what you've done," Sis said.

And Bridgey started, "You'd no right . . ."

Miss Steele said, "I am sorry." The ruler fell to the floor. She handed Zi her handkerchief. "I did not mean to mark you. We must stop fighting among ourselves. Stand back, every one of you. I shall go speak to the miners." She patted her tight hair and swept up her umbrella from its place in the corner. Zi walked after.

She swung around. "I would like to know who you think is in charge here? You sit down and stay there," she said to him in a voice as mean as that first day. When he didn't do as she said she raised her hand to threaten him. "This is my school and my problem, Master Wong Gum Zi. If these men out there think they can bother the brightest pupil I am likely to see in my lifetime, they better think again. Now you get." Zi walked to the farthest corner from everybody and stood there, his head down to hide his tears. "Bridget, when I close the door behind me, you lock it. Do not let Zi out and do not let me in unless I knock like this." She tapped on the wall, tap, tap, stop, tap, tap, stop, tap.

Nora crowded into the corner with Zi and took hold of his hand. I limped over to help Bridgey. When Miss Steele slid through the door, Bridgey was trembling so hard I had to help turn the key. Sis pushed in next to us and laid her ear to the door. For once she had a good idea. We did the same.

"She's standing on the top step scolding at them," Finn called, "with her umbrella up for the rain." We could hear voices outside raised in anger. Something hit the door and Finn said, "They're trying to make her flinch."

Miss Steele hadn't taught above our babble for nothing. Her voice cut through theirs, "You men, just what to you think the job of a teacher is?"

"How do we know, then?" somebody answered.

"I will tell you. It is to protect your children while

they are in my care, to teach them, and to see to their behavior. Your children, Sir, could do with more washing and less fighting." Another rock hit the door.

"Mr. Volk," Miss Steele went on, "this rabble is scaring Annie. I wish you would go along."

"We've not come for a report on our kids, lady. We're after that heathen."

"Is that your father's voice?" Sis whispered.

"Of course not," Bridgey said. "Were Da there, they'd be inside by now."

"Send out that foreign kid," different voices said together.

"Foreign?" Miss Steele asked them. I could tell by the way she clipped her words how mad she was. "Is there a one of you here who is not foreign?"

"We ain't Chinese. We ain't yellow."

"Yellow is exactly what you are," we heard her say. "All of you against one child."

A voice rang out, "Let's see how she looks strung up by her bootlaces."

Finn called, "She's backing up. She's got her umbrella closed and aimed at them like 'tis one of them swords one of them knights carried in one of them magazine stories." What if she couldn't hold them off? I swooped up that terrible ruler and handed it to Cedric and went and stood with Zi. Mr. McMinn would expect me to make a good showing should it come to a battle with the miners.

112

A shout of laughter rose outside. "They're taunting her," Finn said.

And Sis added, "They said, 'See the biddy hen trying to save her chicks' and she shouted that they're all drunk and ought to be ashamed." There came Teacher's pattern of knocks on the door. Bridgey whipped it open and closed and locked in a wink. The girls ran and put their arms around Miss Steele and they leaned on each other and cried. Even Sis.

All Miss Steele's starch was gone and her tight hair hung in wet straggles. "They laughed at me," she sobbed like that was the worst thing that happened.

"Some are scratching their heads," Finn called out. And later: "They're disputing." And later still: "They're all around the pine tree, drinking."

Hedda said, "My pop's kindly to us kids when he's been at the bottle. I think me and Annie better go. Our ma'll worry that we're late." Miss Steele let them out. Mrs. Maynard came later. "She's turning her buggy out front. She's got guns strapped on. The miners are slinking off," Finn called out, full of hisself. He'd found something he was good at besides teasing the girls and making us boys cringe.

The teacher let Mrs. Maynard in. "Thank you, Miss Steele, for keeping the children here. Some of the miners were trying to drive the FanTan gamblers and other troublemakers out of camp. They did not dislodge them, too many wanted them to stay. In frustration, they broke into small groups and rioted through camp, running off the worst of the mining sharks and a footpad someone recognized. We are fortunate no one was hanged. I stayed to assure they did not attack Mr. Wong." She looked at Zi so sadly I knew more was to come.

"So everything ended happily after all," Miss Steele said with a sigh like she'd been holding her breath since lunchtime.

"Not entirely," Mrs. Maynard said. "There is one sad loss."

I didn't want to hear it. There'd already been enough bad things happening for one day but Doreen asked, "What?"

"In the scuffle around the house, the birdcage got turned over. White Star is out again." Either Zi was numb or his bird being gone didn't seem as bad as the first time. He just stared at the floor.

"I'll help you look for it," Finn said and all the Brodies nodded in agreement.

Miss Steele glared hard at Cedric till he said, "I could tell you if I see it, I guess."

She transferred her hard look to Jules. "And me," he said.

Mrs. Maynard said, "Come along, Zi dear, you can ride home in the buggy."

"If you do not mind, Ma'am," he said, "I will walk with the others."

"Would you like a ride, Miss Steele?"

"I'll see the children home, thank you."

We got our things and went outside. "It smells like flowers now the rain's stopped," Bridgey said.

"Let's gather some for around Star's cage," Nora said. "They'll fancy it up so, she'll want to come home." The little kids picked flowers all the way to Main Street, Miss Steele keeping them together with her rolled umbrella.

For the first time in weeks, nobody said anything about the Chinese rot.

11

Pie and Problems

I waited at Mrs. Maynard's gate while the kids piled Zi's arms with flowers. As soon as they wandered off home I said, "Now we can get Father Fergus out of jail."

"How?" Zi asked.

"He can say that the one who stole the brooch has flown. Mr. Paunce will think he means one of the sinners the miners chased out of camp today."

Zi asked, "May I go with you to tell him? Come help me strew these flowers around Star's cage first. They really may bring her back."

"If they don't you could always borrow Mrs. Paunce's brooch and hang it out to draw her," I said, so full of excitement at getting Father Fergus free, I could joke about the theft for the first time.

Through the bars in the jail door Father Fergus looked paler than before, and fatter. The Irish and Polish ladies had shared their food with him whenever they had a little extra. People said the marshal's wife fed him up, too, relieved to have a jailbird who'd not try to escape and murder them in their beds. She'd treated him like the mayor of Denver come to visit, even giving him a feather mattress to sleep on.

I told him about White Star getting loose. You wouldn't think a man who'd been locked in jail could laugh aloud like that. "You two got me in and you're going to get me out," he said. "I'm grateful. I've had enough of the bishop's solitude. And you've provided an out for Mr. Paunce, too. He knew I could never tell him what had been revealed to me in secret, but he didn't think of all the trouble he'd cause by demanding it. You run along now. When the marshal brings me my supper, I'll tell him to let Mr. Paunce know I'm ready to talk."

"Will you tell that Star was the thief?" Zi asked.

"No, only that the one who stole the brooch is no longer a threat to Miner's Chance. I like your way of putting it, Renny, 'The thief has flown.' That will satisfy him. Poor man, he caught his foot in his own trap when he put me in here. He's lost a sack of money on the strike. But you get that bird caged and keep him locked up from now on, you hear?"

Zi nodded and we started toward Mrs. Maynard's but the priest called us back. "The name of the true thief had best be our secret forever, don't you think?" We agreed and ran off whooping.

"I thought you were sad about that bird," Sis said when she met us on the path. All we could do was grin.

As I walked home near her tiny house, Miss Hettie

called me over and handed me a pie. "Where do you want it delivered?" I asked her.

"Nowhere. Take it to your family. 'Tis one I couldn't sell. The strike is even hitting the pie business."

I thanked her and thanked her. We'd never have money to spend on one of her pies. "It smells like apple," I said.

"That's what 'tis, from my own dried store of them."

"'Twill make a feast." There was more to it than just a good smell. 'Twas what Nora meant when she talked about *MissHettiesbeautifulpies* like that was all one word. Up close the crust was a wonder, decorated with scrolls and swirls in tiny slits that wound in and out making patterns. Proud, I carried it home.

When I went in our cabin and told about the pie it raised a hullabaloo. Mam thought to cut it right then but Nora shrieked, "Don't anybody eat it."

"Your da won't mind. We'll save him some," Mam said.

Nora stamped her feet. "Don't eat it. Don't you eat it."

"What's the matter?" Bridgey asked. "You'd think 'twas made of cat."

"'Tis worse," Nora said. "'Tis how she makes the designs."

"What do you mean?"

"I went in early and she was doing it. Ugh. It makes me sick to think on it."

"Don't tell me you're going to throw up," Mam said, "because you're not."

"What's so terrible about how she decorates them?" Bridgey asked her.

"She has those big fake-looking, shiny, white teeth. She takes them out and prints circles and things."

Bridgey bent over the pie. "Of course. You can see. 'Tis a wonder nobody guessed that."

"Don't you say a word about it, Nora," Mam said. "Not to anyone. 'Tis the only way the old dear has to make money."

Bridgey laughed so she could hardly talk. "I don't care how she does it. She cooks them after. Serve me some."

"Well, you may not care but I do," Mam said, laughing, too. "Here, Renny. Put it out by the shed. Some animal will come eat it." That bear, I thought, or a lion. But I did as Mam said.

Da came home mad because the miners rampaged through the camp without waiting for him to explain his plan. If they'd done it his way, he said, the gambling tent would be gone. When he came across that perfect pie on his way past the shed it added to his anger. He grabbed it up and stormed in demanding, "What is this waste of food?"

Mam explained about Miss Hettie's teeth. She had a way of soothing Da's anger, getting him to see the funny side of things. She praised him, too, saying how grand she thought him, leading the miners in trying to rid the camp of scoundrels. "Don't brag on me yet," Da said. "I'll get it done. But not unless I pick my men and do it on the quiet."

Our door swung open and the Brodie twins came in, so young they didn't think of knocking. "Can our mam have another bowl of meal?" Mayo asked. Mam took the bowl and went to fill it.

"Ay, and what's this?" Da asked.

"A little charity," Mam said, "because of the strike."

"And do I wear away my life in the mine, then, to feed the neighbors?"

"Hush you," Mam said, nodding toward Mayo and Mab as she pushed them out the door with their full bowl.

But Da'd started and wasn't to be stopped. "Charity is for the rich, not for us. You'd let all I've worked for trickle away in kindness."

"I thought you'd come home proud and great-hearted, having spent your day chasing sinners from the camp."

"I would have, had the job been done right. But I'll not rest till 'tis finished. Especially not before those Wongs are gone. You know why we didn't get them out this afternoon?" Mam shook her head. "Because that Mrs. Maynard showed her guns between the miners and the da. The boy was at school and that beanpole teacher drove off the men that went up there."

"Miss Steele did that?" Mam asked us.

"With her umbrella." Bridgey laughed.

"It wasn't funny," I said. "They tried to beat down the

door and threw rocks and threatened to hang Teacher upside down. It scared the little kids something awful."

Bridgey said, "You should have seen Zi. He acted really brave, wanting to give hisself up lest the rest of us get hurt."

"You sound like you're braggin' on him," Da said in his most biting voice.

"I'm only saying what happened," Bridgey bit back.

He turned to me. "You'll have no more to do with that Chinaman, for money or any other reason. If that widow woman is so set on running things, let her care for him herself."

"Why, Da?" I asked. Though I knew 'twas to spite Mrs. Maynard.

"You ought to be scrapping in the street with the other boys. Not hanging around with him. You shame me, acting so."

"I promised I'd walk him home till school ends."

He flicked his hand as though to brush my answer away. "That's one promise you've kept long enough."

"But he's my friend." I'd said it out at last. I expected lightning to strike. It didn't for a minute.

"And how would it sound were your mam to write in her letter home to Ireland, 'Renny is friends with a Chinaman?' They'd think our trip across the ocean addled our brains."

"I don't care what they'd think." Before I knew what he was planning, his fist caught me and my head crashed back against the log wall. Nora screamed. I pressed my head between my hands to stop it ringing. Blood seeped between my fingers.

"You girls get to the loft. Now!" Da said. Bridgey scampered up the ladder sniffling.

Nora clung to me, "Don't you hit my Renny."

"Get along with Bridgey," I said, as scared for her as for me. Da ranted a lot but he didn't let hisself go often. When he did, we scattered.

But Nora didn't go. "You oughtn't to act so mean. Except for him, those bears would have ate me." She gave me one frightened look and scampered up the ladder spouting tears. The rest stood silent, like they waited for something terrible to happen.

At last Da said, "What bears?"

"Some we met on the way to school," I said.

"You took Nora by the shortcut in April?"

"We were late."

"Had you been a day late, a week late, you shouldn't have gone that way." He struck me again.

I stood straight to receive his blow. I'd been carrying the secret of the bears like a great stone. His hitting me seemed just, made the stone weigh a little lighter. "You're right to hate me about the bears," I said aloud. To myself I said, 'But not about Zi.'

"He doesn't hate you," Mam said, though she gave Da a dreadful look. "Love and hate look a lot alike sometimes." She stroked my hair back to see how bad my head was cut.

"You stand away, Peg," Da said. "This is between him

122

and me. It's been coming. I'll make a man of him or break him."

"Break me then. I'll never be the bully you want."

"You're likely right and a sad day 'tis you admitting it."

"Hush," Mam said. "The two of you are just the same. Stubborn as mules."

"Me like him?" Da laughed in a scornful way. "He's feeble as porridge with no salt."

"And so were you at his age. Were you as hard then as you want him to be, those days wouldn't haunt you so."

"I bade you not to speak of that time. Never was I soft like him. See him cry for being hit a little."

"He'll learn to be tough when he needs to. Though not if you drum at him all the time about it. Don't drive kindness out of the lad. 'Tis bad enough you try to stamp it out in yourself."

"People like us can't afford to be kind," Da said.

"People like us . . ." I started.

"Hush you, both of you," Mam said. "Unless you two find a way to rub along together, this family'll start unraveling like one of Bridget's knit stockings when she's careless with her needles." She put the supper on and called the girls down and we sat around the table without talking. Except for Da, nobody ate much.

Only he made a feast of Miss Hettie's pie.

12

Night Hunting

Sometime in the night Da woke me. "Get yourself dressed," he muttered, "we're going hunting."

I leapt up. Da knew I loved hunting with him, leaving home in the night, tracking through woods for elk or deer or wild turkeys as the sky grayed to dawn. He must be wanting to make up our differences.

He'd already climbed back down the ladder so I couldn't ask where we were headed. I missed the smell of coffee and porridge Mam usually had ready for us. No lamp was lit, either. As I reached the bottom of the ladder he hissed, "Be silent."

Mam's sleepy voice came through the dark, "Lon?" Da opened the door for us to go out and shut it against her questions. He led me into the shed and shoved something in my hand. "Rub this charcoal over your hands and face so you'll not be knowed." He began rubbing some on hisself.

"Knowed by the elk?" I asked half joking, half puzzled.

"'Tis not elk we're after this time. Hurry up."

"What about the gun?" I asked.

"Stout clubs will be enough. Gunshots would bring questions from folk who'd try to stop what we're doing. We'll move in silence. Remember that." It got me mad, him making such a secret of what we were about.

Men waited on the path that ran from the top of Irish Gulch. So hard were they to see against the dark, I knew their hands and faces must be blacked like ours. "What's this, then, Lon," one said, "you've brought the boy?"

"As you see," Da said.

"These won't be sights a kid that young should look upon," another said. Mr. Brodie 'twas. I'd never known he gave a thought to kids.

"He'll carry the torch," Da said.

"'Tis not right, you bringing him."

"'Tis for his good," Da said. "He's had it easy too long. Either the both of us go or the both of us stay." That decided it. "To the FanTan tent then."

They argued plans in whispers. "I could cut the guy ropes and the tent would go down." That was Finn's voice! So he was one of them.

"Do it and the tent will go down sure enough. Right on the stove and the whole gulch goes up in flames." Disgust burned in Da's voice at Finn's foolishness.

We moved down to where the church stood almost finished. Da said to me, "This part you stay out of. Lean there against the church and watch. You'll see what a man has to do to clear a camp of criminals and make it safe for his kids." He crouched down so his eyes peered into mine. "Though things turn ugly, don't let that soft heart of yours take over. You turn tail and run and you're no son of mine! I'll bar our door against you. Forever." Then his voice softened. "Do as you're bade tonight and we'll forget our quarrel."

"Well, sure, Da," I said, wanting to put our bad feelings behind us.

The moon ran through thin clouds showing every wrinkle in that shiny tent. A murmur rose from inside it and laughter. "We'll move in silence," Da told the others. "We don't want to be known by our voices." They pushed inside. I heard the thump of their clubs smashing things. Panel after panel of the tent split open where somebody slashed with a long knife. The little flags on top fluttered like in a wind.

Protests swelled as the Chinese tried to protect what was theirs. Through one of the slashes shone a red glow from the open door of the stove. Bodies struggled in front of it. Two shots rang and echoed. Da and them never spoke as they thrashed the gamblers and their women toward the Fairplay road. Men from camp fled in the other direction. The sobbing I thought was theirs was mine.

Then I heard Da's voice and Finn's raised in answer. "You'll go on home," Da said.

"What's happened?" somebody asked.

"He near killed that man, the young devil. Beat him full force like he was driving a fence post into hard ground. He'll get us all hauled in for murder."

"I didn't mean it," Finn said.

"I'd be by-God-angry to be beat to death by some-body who didn't mean it. You go on home. You're not to be trusted with a club in your hands."

Mr. Brodie spoke for Finn but Da wasn't having any of it. "I'll not go on with him along. He'll get us strung up by our necks." They thought enough of him not to argue.

Except Finn. "Give me another chance," he begged.

"I'll give you another chance when your sense has caught up to your muscle. Not tonight." Finn, hunched like he'd been struck, started back up the gulch path.

"I've got their money box," somebody called.

"Leave it for the marshal," Da said. "We're not out to steal. When Paunce said 'It's time all in the camp start keeping the law' he meant all but hisself. We'll show him what real law and order looks like." We walked away, the FanTan tent in a heap behind us. My fears quieted a little. If 'twas law and order they sought, maybe they'd let the law-abiding Wongs alone.

Somebody asked, "Where to next?"

"Two girls at the Gilded Lily are said to be lifting gold dust pouches off their customers. Emmaline and Trixie. We'll want a torch for this." Da set it afire and gave it to me to hold. I tensed again, wondering if they'd club the girls like they did the gamblers.

The girls lived where I'd left the pups. Lights shone from the windows. Two of our men slipped around back in case people tried to pour out that way. Mr. Brodie knocked at the front door. A woman opened it. Her dress was a shining blue. The plume in her hair curved down over her shoulder and across her front. I'd have to tell Bridgey how fancy that made her look.

Our blackened faces and hands must have warned her to be wary. "What do you want?" she asked.

"We're here for Emmaline and Trixie," Mr. Brodie said.

"You want them for what?"

"They've stole. They've five minutes to pack and get out here," he said.

"Maybe Emmaline," she said. "But Trixie's a good kid."

"We're not here to talk things over, 'tis all decided," Da called.

"And if they won't come?"

"See the torch the boy holds? He'll set the house afire with it." I began to shake so bad the flame trembled and circled.

She turned slow as if our demands caused no alarm. But she forgot to close the door. I saw the excitement we'd caused inside. People ran back and forth as agitated as the pack rat babies when I turned over their nest. Dogs barked. Two girls were pushed onto the steps, one not much older than Bridgey. They held valises like they meant to catch the stage.

Mr. Brodie tipped his cap, his forehead and ear tops showing white where he'd not charcoaled. "We're sending you on your way to Fairplay, Misses. We can't let thieves stay in camp. 'Tis best you wait for daylight to take the shelf road lest you stray over the edge in the dark."

Behind me Da grumbled, "He's wasting time treating them like ladies." The younger girl struggled not to cry. The older spat at Mr. Brodie's feet.

I pulled Da's sleeve. "What if she didn't steal, Da, that Trixie?" I felt the girls' eyes on me, me who was expected to set their house afire.

"You're here to watch, not question," he said.

The girls set off with a man following to see they didn't turn back. Da ground the torch out in the dust of the road. We trailed down Main Street.

The dentist sat on one of his barrels waiting for business. Da and the others talked with him, the night eyes of Miner's Chance, seeing all that went on. He told where a pickpocket slept and said somebody new in camp was rumored to be a cutthroat. They went and routed them out and beat them bad so they'd not relish coming back. My stomach turned over and my throat burned. What they were doing was too chancy. Maybe the night dentist was wrong and the man he called a cutthroat wasn't one. If this was law and order I was against it.

"I could stand some whiskey," Mr. Brodie said.

"Whiskey ruined our plans this afternoon," Da said.

"I'm dry-tongued as a pup in August. I can't carry on without some," Mr. Brodie insisted. Da didn't give him the satisfaction of a answer.

Somebody reminded, "There's the priest yet to let loose." They hurried to the jail and set to gouging at the lock with a knife.

When the door swung in, Da went inside. Soon he came out. "He's not coming away with us. He says it wasn't right, us breaking into the jail. Isn't happy that we're out cleaning up the camp, either. Said beating people with clubs is no way to convince them." Da sounded angry.

Mr. Brodie asked, "I thought them Chinese gamblers looked pretty convinced, didn't you?"

Somebody else asked, "Where's his thankfulness? Didn't we give up our pay, our families crying for food, for his sake?"

Father Fergus came to the door of his cell in a gray nightshirt. "I'm grateful for your strike. More grateful than I can say. The pain you and your families suffered for my sake was a holy thing. But if I break out of jail without the marshal's say-so, a slinking runaway, the good of the strike will be lost. We'll be no closer to law and order than before."

That didn't please the men. Maybe they didn't understand what he meant. They hadn't heard the homily he'd given me on law and order.

He must have seen they were angry. "This is how I see it," he said. "Paunce slaps me in jail. That doesn't make me tell who stole the brooch. You strike thinking he'll let me go. But he doesn't. We're in a fix there's no way out of. But something starts slow, like ice breaking up on the creek. One man comes in the night and asks me, "What's to be done to break Paunce's power since the strike isn't doing it?" Another comes, and another. Every night the crowd gets bigger; shopkeepers, drivers, repairmen, bartenders, clerks, talking together about how this camp could be run better. The outcome of your strike will be a peaceful and law-abiding camp. That's something I've prayed for."

But Da wasn't interested in Father Fergus's kind of peace and lawfulness. He said to the others, "Then there's just those Chinese Wongs left to take care of. That done we can go home and sleep the sleep of the just." No, I wanted to scream, No!

Father Fergus and I looked into each other's eyes through the crowd but he gave no sign. "What's this about the Wongs?" he asked.

"They've got to go," Da said.

"What harm are they?" asked the priest.

"They're like a magnet to six-penny nails. Already other Chinese have followed them into the camp and look at the trouble they've caused! We should have drove them out the day they arrived," Da said.

Those were the last words I caught. Voices murmured on as I stepped back till I could turn and run. I threw the torch off into the dark lest they relight it to fire the carriage house where Zi and his da slept.

I thought Da's feet came pounding after me but 'twas only my heart. "Don't run off though things turn ugly. You do and you're no son of mine!" my mind said over and over as I ran. I knew Da meant it. But I couldn't let them batter Zi and his da like they'd done those others.

I banged on the door at Mrs. Maynard's and almost fell inside, it opened so fast. She stood holding a gun, a lamp glimmering behind her. "Quick," I said as best I could for panting, "they're coming for Zi and his da."

"I thought they might since they failed today. Come in. I have brought the Wongs here for the night. You will be safe here, too."

I shook my head, needing to be gone before Da came. I said, "Most of them took no pleasure in what they felt they'd got to do tonight. Maybe they'll listen to reason."

"You are a fine boy, young Renny," she said. "I owe you more than I can ever repay and so do others." She bent and kissed me before she closed the door.

I could run no further. My breath came in gasps. A bush inside the picket fence offered a place to hide. Though barely budding, its down-curving branches made a cave. I crawled under and lay still as a stone lest Da see me when he came and know I'd betrayed him, warning Mrs. Maynard.

Soon they came straggling up the path from Main Street. As Da swung open her gate Mrs. Maynard stepped onto the porch. "Come no further," she said. She wasn't dressed plain that time. She wore a black fur wrap that touched the floor and caught the gleam of the moon. So she'd spent some money on show after all! It would make it harder for them to scorn her, her get-up announcing how rich and important she was.

"We're cleaning the camp of sinners tonight," Da said.

"I see you have not been cleaning yourselves," she said as snappish as Miss Steele for once.

Mr. Brodie rubbed his black hands on his black pants. "We'll just step around to the carriage house, Ma'am," he said like 'twas a apology.

"No, you will not set foot inside my fence. There are no sinners here. If you are mistakenly thinking to include the Wongs in your cleanup, be warned. I am committed to keeping them safe."

"And how will you do that?" Da asked. He swung his club up where she could see it.

"Like this." She raised her revolver and it clicked as she cocked it. The lantern the Paunces kept lighted to show off their metal fountain shattered with her bullet. She swung the gun back so it menaced the men. It clicked again. "There is a better way than this to settle our differences if you will listen," she said. There came a mumbling as some said yes and some said no. "I agree not to hire Chinese labor at the Rejoice as long as the Wongs are left alone."

"You'll write that for us on a paper?" Mr. Brodie asked.

"I will," she said. "However, if they are driven from camp, I shall close the mine and leave Miner's Chance. We all know how many mining families would be hurt by your forcing me to do that. I shall publicize that it was your doing, not mine."

"Your plan helps your own miners, not us," Da said.

"If we turn our backs at the Kitkat, Paunce will be there with Chinese to take our place."

"From what I hear of you, Mr. Sholto, you can prevent his bringing them in. If you cannot, give in your names at my office. I am always eager to hire skilled miners." They stood shuffling their feet. Then they bunched together and disputed and their hands flew. I guessed Da was telling them not to give in to a woman. He'd hate working for one, even one who'd played fairer with them than their own boss. In the end, what could they do but what she asked? They walked off one by one.

Da stayed, the moon casting sharp shadows of him, the fence and the trees. "You're ruining my boy," he told her.

"How am I ruining him?"

"He's spent the spring hanging around your Chink kid instead of his own people. It's set the camp against him and him against me, his own da."

"You should be proud, one standing alone against so many. I asked him because I thought he could. He is the strongest boy in the school."

"He's never. Finn is."

"All Finn has is brute strength, which wins only until the next stronger comes along. Renny acts from his heart."

"I see you know him well," my da said and he laughed. 'Twas the bitter kind of laugh that makes you ache to hear. "Heart breaks a boy in the mines. He'll be one of those that hates crouching in the wet dark, no more regarded than the rats that fight him for his lunch. He'll see danger in every creak of the timbers, quail if a rock drops. Yet he'll act the hero when there's accidents and he ought to be saving hisself for the sake of his family."

"You exaggerate about the rats," she said. And when he didn't deny it, "Has it never occurred to you that he may not go into the mines?"

"And where else would a miner's boy go, then, to make his living?" he asked her as exasperated as though she was Nora asking a dumb question.

He turned away, not waiting for her answer but she shouted it after him anyway. "You speak so clearly of how it will feel to him in the mine. I wonder if that does not mean you are a person of heart yourself?" He went on walking. Could she be right about him, that he was a man of heart? If he was, maybe Mam had been right when she said he was harsh with me because he wanted the best for me. And when she said love and hate look a lot alike sometimes. I longed to run after and ask him if Mam spoke true. But I didn't. I was too afraid of his answer.

Mrs. Maynard lowered her revolver and went inside. The door shut and the lock snapped. So Zi'd stay and get his chance to learn to be a American boy! As for me, Da was on his way home to shut our door and bar it against me.

Forever.

13

Fire!

A feeling of danger woke me. I yawned and stretched, surprised to find myself, dappled by moonlight, still under the thimbleberry bush in the corner of Mrs. Maynard's front fence. But where else would you be, I asked myself, Da saying you were no son of his, gone home to bar the door against you? What else would you feel but danger?

There was a glow beyond the house. I watched it deepen, taking it for sunrise till I was full awake. Then I leapt to my feet and ran. The light came from the wrong place for either dawn or moonset. I heard crackling and smelled smoke. Close by me the bays whinnied and plunged in their stalls. Ahead firelight shone through cracks in the carriage house door.

I opened the top half of the stable door and sought to soothe the horses, crooning as I did when I groomed them. They were smoke crazed and one reared, his hooves raking the wall as he set down. I daren't approach. I swung the lower door back and they fled out and up through the canyon. As I watched them go, willing they'd not break a leg in a badger hole, White Star scared me flapping past, dripping flower petals. "Renny," she squawked with alarm, "Renny," and disappeared like the horses into the dark.

I pounded on the back door of the big house, then ran to the carriage house door, opened it a crack and slipped through. Smoke seared my throat and eyes. "Oh, God, Renny, help." 'Twas Finn striking at the blazing green sleigh with a gunnysack. Fire had already eaten half the carriage that stood farther back.

"There's more sacks there." He pointed. I grabbed one and lashed at the flames. "I thought to smoke out the Wongs. Show your da I can do things right. Make him sorry he drove me off." He coughed and a sob caught his throat. "It turned to flaming, not smoking. Maybe I used too much hay. The whole canyon could go."

"We can't stop it alone," I gasped, trying to figure what to do, trying to use my head. "'Tis too far along. We need the fire brigade with their pumper. Run tell them to come."

"I daren't," he said. "They'd outlaw a kid that set a fire."

"Go to the top of the path. Shout 'Fire' down to the boardwalk till somebody rings the bell. Don't show yourself."

He took a few more swipes at the fire. "I'll meet the brigade as they come. Nobody need know." He pounded away.

I flailed at the flames, thinking of the Wongs' beautiful scrolls and stitched pictures upstairs above me maybe already curled with the heat. 'Twas all they owned. I went harder at the fire, trampling with my boots, striking with my hands, beating with sacks. The fire bell began to clang.

Then Mr. Wong was fighting beside me. Zi came running with water and we dipped sacks in and smote the fire. Three servants ran over from the Paunces' in their nightclothes and brought pails from the well to empty on the flames.

The fire brigade came at last. I knew they'd got there when Da shook my shoulder and shouted to get back. Wheezing and pulling their pump cart, the men got it set as Da directed them and pointed the hose toward the fire. I sank on the back steps of the big house and stared at the ground. My hands ached like they were aflame. I swallowed and swallowed not to throw up.

Zi dropped down beside me, his front hair frizzed brown on black, his pigtail the same. He heaved like he'd never get a full breath. Mr. Wong came toward us. He laid his hands on our heads. "Ask your da has smoke ruint the things upstairs," I told Zi. They talked together.

"They are unharmed because of you. Will just need airing. We thank you ten times, a hundred times, a thousand times." His mouth curled like when he was making a joke but I could tell he was serious. 'Twas glad news and good luck. The upstairs could have ended like the downstairs where the skeletons of the carriage and sleigh smoked in a mess of ash and water.

When the fire was no more than a smolder, Mrs. Maynard called Zi and Mr. Wong in to help her lay out food for the brigade. "Perhaps you would do better to leave your boots outside," she told the firefighters. I bent down to untie mine. My hands were burnt too bad. My fingers wouldn't bend.

"Aren't you coming in?" Mr. Brodie asked as he mounted the steps. Da came behind him.

"I can't get off my boots."

Da knelt down and unlaced them and slid them off. He turned my hands over to see the burns. "'Tis all right to cry."

"It wouldn't help, crying. They're burned too bad," I said and knew I'd cried at hurts for the last time. "I didn't run off from you because I was too weak-hearted to watch what you did. I was proud you wanted to clean up the camp. I ran off to warn Mrs. Maynard lest Zi and Mr. Wong got clubbed like those others. I guess to you that's just as bad."

He made no answer to that but said, "It was a waste, you fighting the fire like all depended on you. The brigade got here in time to keep it from spreading."

"Not in time to save the upstairs. All Zi and his da have is up there. Things they mean to sell to get Zi a education." He shook his head like he'd never understand me but he helped me up.

The firefighters stood around the dining room eating

ham sandwiches and drinking coffee. Mr. McMinn was there, and Mr. Brodie, making jokes, and miners from the Kitkat. They boasted to each other how fast they'd come and how quick they'd doused the flames. One by one they shook Finn's hand, it being the first fire he'd fought with them. Mr. Wong passed among them with cake Mrs. Paunce sent over. Nobody paid him any mind like Chinese were something they'd got used to.

Zi ran for Dr. Applegate and while we waited Mrs. Maynard helped me ease off my coat. "I am worried about you, Renny Sholto," she said. "Will I ever see you that you do not look more battered than the time before? Will I ever find a way to thank you for all you've done for me?"

I'd like to have told her this might be our last talk. If Da still thought I was no son of his, I'd push off to Fairplay to try to make my own way. It wouldn't do to stay in camp, a living shame to the miners' hero.

The doctor came then. I wasn't the only one needing his attention. Mr. Wong had leg burns and Zi a scorched arm. One of the brigade had a cinder in his eye. When Dr. Applegate got to me he said, "You won't be writing for your teacher or working with the horses or boxing McMinn for awhile." It warmed me, him knowing all those things about me though we'd never spoke before.

"You were there before the fire brigade, they say," he went on. "How did the fire start?" The room quieted so all could catch my answer. Finn shrank back against the wall, waiting for the terrible truth to come out.

Should I guard his secret? I wished Father Fergus was there to ask. "I didn't see it start," I said. "I'd caught a catnap under a bush, tired from being out late. The firelight woke me. I heard the horses thrash around and let them go. By then Mr. Wong and Zi came and some of Mr. Paunce's people to help."

I'd done it again. I'd taken on Finn like before I'd taken on Zi. Bridgey's question echoed in my head, "Why do you always try to save everybody?" I still didn't know the answer.

Them that fought the fire gathered around and watched the doctor work over my hands. It was different from the time at the Green Eyes when they acted like I was some criminal and them my judges. This night I was one of their own. "You should see him fight," Mr. McMinn said. "Any day now he'll flatten me on the floor." They looked at my burns like they were medals I'd won.

"He's a good, feisty, Irish boy," somebody said to Da. "You can be proud."

Da rocked back and forth on his feet and didn't give a answer. I felt he knew, somehow, I'd lied for Finn. "Renny," he said, at last, like he'd been making up his mind, "we better go." Go where? I wondered. He put my coat around me and buttoned one button to stop it sliding off.

Everybody started away. Mrs. Maynard waved, Zi and his da smiling from the shadows behind her. The brigade went first, in and out of pockets of smoke, larking and capering, made foolish by their victory over the fire.

Da and me walked slow not to joggle my hands too much, silent. I was trying to make sense of all that happened. At last Da spoke. "Finn started the fire, didn't he?"

I thought of trying to slide past the truth but could see Da was not to be duped. "How did you know?" I asked.

"The young fool. Here he comes running to join the rest of us, sly-faced and hangdog, smelling like he'd been pickled in wood smoke. 'Twas clear he'd been up to something. What did he do?"

Again I thought to shade the truth but instead I told him. When I got through he asked, "Why lie for him?"

"I didn't lie. I just didn't tell it all."

"'Tis the same thing. Why shield him?"

"I don't know. Maybe 'twas something Mr. Wong said. That Finn was owed pity because the camp's shoved him to the bottom and might always hold him there and he's afraid."

"Crazy Chinese foolery." He didn't say it wasn't true. "I don't know about you and Finn, you boys maybe ought to be drowned in the creek to save the camp." He didn't sound like he meant it. I wondered if that was like my joke about hanging the brooch out to get Star back, a feeling of silliness after a long, bad time.

Whatever it meant, he was talking to me like a equal, the way he did with friends at the Green Eyes. The testiness was gone from his answers, and the frown I'd got so used to. Something new had slid in place between us. Maybe I wasn't going to fail him after all.

'Twas the time between late night and first morning when the marshal would have arrested Father Fergus if he'd had enough sense. We walked up the middle of the wide street. Those that were still in the saloons and Gambler Jim's and the dance hall came out on the boardwalks to cheer the brigade.

As we passed the Spiffy Gent, they raised their glasses and said, "To Lon Sholto, brigade captain."

But Da put up his hand to stop them and said, "Here's the one deserves your toast. Were it not for him finding the fire, and fighting it till we came, this whole side of the canyon would be ashes."

"Who is he then," one of them asked, "that we can call out his name?"

"He's my own son. His name's Renny." They raised their glasses and clinked them together and my name bounced back and forth across the street. It felt like getting all the arithmetic problems right or being writ up in the newspaper. But what was better was Da standing there proud, smiling that special smile at me that always set things right with people.

It set them right with me.